WHO WILL BUILD THE NATION?

By Mordechai Kofi Amofa

To God Be The Glory

WHO WILL BUILD THE NATION

ISBN: 9789988545581

Published By
DERECH COMMUNICATIONS
P.O.Box GP 4925, Accra
Tel: 233(0) 242652082
Email: derechcommunications@gmail.com

For further enquiries,
Contact the author on Tel: 233(0) 242652082
Email: sirmordechai613@gmail.com

Designed & Printed By
Print Palace Ghana
P.O.Box KT 441 , Kotobabi Accra- Ghana
Tel: 233(0)241032450
Email: ppgghana@gmail.com

All names, places and institutions mentioned in this book are a product of the author's imagination.

This book is specially dedicated to my mother; Martha Adwoa Korkoa, my aunt; Maame Yaa Tawiah and my daughter; Eliana Esi Korkoa Amofa.

This book is also dedicated to all living and departed patriots of all nations.

Acknowledgements

Glory be to God, the creator of all for the inspiration that fueled this project.

It is difficult to mention names of all who have made this book a success. However, the assistance of my wife, Joana Otoo, who has been a solid pillar behind this wonderful work cannot be forgotten. Also the unwavering support received from Mr. Isaac Adokwei Acquaye, a brother from another mother has been very monumental.

I sincerely thank Professor Ebenezer Oduro Owusu, Vice Chancellor of University of Ghana for graciously accepting to write the foreword to this book in spite of his very busy schedule.

I thank Mrs. Naa Leyoo Watson Nortey (Lecturer, African University College of Communications) and Mr. Nketiah Kyeremeh (MA) for selflessly reviewing the book on time and providing useful suggestions.

I must thank Mrs. Ohui Allotey, Editor, Ghana Book Publishing Council for her speedy editing of the manuscript.

I am also grateful to Mr. Francis Kuadzi who designed this book.

I cannot forget the contributions of the following

notable persons for their various pivotal roles; Messrs Bonito Olympio Sylvanus,John Tetteh Hogrey, Kwasi Dwamena Oware, Henry Harding, Daniel Yeboah, Amos Awortwe, Raphael Boadu, Robert Mawuli Fialor, Joseph Danquah, Charles Darkwa and Patrick Ashia.

Foreword

For the kingdom is the Lord's: And He rules over the nations. (Psalm 22:28 KJV)

"Who Will Build the Nation" emphasizes the importance of laws, which govern a state, and consequences of the poor enforcement of the laws in national developmental efforts.

This book addresses the issues we witness and encounter in our societies every day; power play and intimidation, indiscipline, breakdown of law and order, unproductive attitudes, and the blatant abuses of our rights to speech and freedom of the media.

The book again talks about the very important role journalists play in promoting the peace of the country, and how passion-driven leaders who genuinely have the interests of the country at heart can build the nation. Leadership should be centred on protecting citizens, inspiring hope (especially to the hopeless), and instituting the true meaning of life to the betterment of the citizenry.
The perceived level of spirituality of a nation does not necessarily determine the progress of that nation. Hate and vengeful rivalry destroy a nation; misinformation leads to violence and deters

progress, while love, unity, truth and respect develop a nation. Religion and politics must aim at serving humanity and not exploiting them. Politics is not necessarily a dirty game. It is the mode of play which determines its state. The intention of serving humanity and creating a better world for posterity makes it a game worth playing.

We long for financial independence, but greed has made that impossible leading to illegal activities causing retardation in the progress of our nation and eventual destruction. It is about time to reclaim and rebuild our nation. If we fail to do so this time, doom awaits us forever !

In rebuilding our nation, discipline, truthfulness, and the rule of law must prevail at all levels. The law is meant for all irrespective of one's spiritual or political status. No one is above the law. Thus, religion/culture cannot be a justification for lawlessness.

I believe this book, 'Who Will Build the Nation' is a must-have for everyone; the political and religious leader, the journalist who has listeners all over the country, and the citizen who has the interest of the nation at heart.

It is my hope that by reading this book, our hearts will be touched, and we will have a mindset that allows us to place the interest of our nation ahead of all others, in all endeavours. We need to be truthful and patriotic in seeking a turn to rebuild

our nation Ghana.
Let us learn to serve the people, our country and God with pride, truth, dignity and integrity!

Professor Ebenezer Oduro Owusu
Vice Chancellor
University of Ghana

INTRODUCTION

This literary fiction probes the critical question, who will build the nation? The novel adequately discusses the responsibilities that citizens have to shoulder in their quest to build the nation.

Since chaos and anarchy have torn many hitherto stable nations apart, the narrative craftily encourages media and political actors to promote national cohesion, decency in public discourse and Integrity in public life.

It also educates the reader to use peaceful means in resolving societal issues because, "Anger and violence have courted many to commit crimes they never intended."

The story is fascinating, relevant and educative and will serve as a useful material for promoting the rule of law and national cohesion.

"You don't need to be tolerant of those who share your opinions, or whose behaviour you approve. It is when we are angry that we most need to apply our proclaimed principles of humility and mutual respect." – ***Kofi Annan, a former UN Secretary General.***

Sometimes, in our hurry to break the news, we break hearts,
Sometimes, in our zeal to gain considerable attention,
we cause irreparable destruction,
Comrades of media and politics, you owe a duty to society,
What you say, what you write, shall not escape the scrutiny of posterity,
Fan not the sentiments that divide us and fray not the bonds that bind us,
or else, we will fall apart!
The clock is ticking, duty is calling, generations are expecting,
Who will build the nation?

CHAPTER ONE

Susubribi walked to the stage amidst resounding applause from the ecstatic audience. With assuring confidence and a smile, he mounted the podium and waved at the audience as he looked across the packed auditorium. He saw his aide running up to him just as he was about to make his opening remarks. He lowered his head and listened as the aide approached and whispered in his ear. The brightness in his face dimmed and the smile he wore moments ago disappeared. He was stricken into stillness by the looming danger as he stood and stared at the dignitaries who were equally puzzled.

One could hear rumblings of discontent among the audience and the faces that had been radiant with excitement were now dull. Susubribi had been invited by the Conference of University Student Leaders to give the keynote address but what he heard meant he had to leave the stage without delay.

'You must have heard the unfortunate news that just came in,' he announced after conferring with the dignitaries. 'An eruption of political violence in the city is reported to have resulted in loss of lives and property. Rapid deployment of police to calm the situation was not successful and we understand the violent youth are dispensing their energies on mindless brutalities. We gather that the situation could escalate if the security agencies are unable to swiftly restrain the mob. It is feared we may suffer heavy casualties,' he revealed.

'In recent times,' he continued, 'we have been tottering on the brink of instability and the threat of violence is more real than imagined. It seems we have reached a stage where the fear of external aggression is less threatening than the internal acrimony that stares us in the face. The air is getting thicker with hostility as certain utterances continue to tear apart the garment of national unity. Is there an end in sight for religious and political conflicts in Masem? Will the aggressive pursuit of power wreck the ship of state or, will the zealous expression of our faiths endanger our fate?'

'Good citizens desire to live in a peaceful and stable society where the rule of law is supreme. They passionately conduct their affairs in a manner that promotes goodwill, patriotism, unity and a harmonious society. They are not cynical bystanders who look on and complain but ardent optimists who are motivated by what is possible.

'As student leaders, you are likely to occupy key positions in society when you leave your various institutions of learning and join the world of work. In whatever field of endeavour, in whatever role or capacity, as responsible citizens, you must always consider; will my politics build the nation or destroy it? Will my occupation build the nation or destroy it? Strive to be among the pearls, known for decency in discourse and probity of conduct. Build your nation and do not destroy it,' Susubribi charged and hurried off the stage.

Leaders of the Integrity Party (IP) at the conference rushed to the party headquarters where a crisis meeting was underway. Deliberations dragged on for hours but a consensus could not be reached because opinions were as divergent as crossroads. Susubribi arrived home late and went to bed but he could not sleep. His eyes were fixed on the clock which seemed to be running at a fast pace, yet daybreak felt like it is travelling on a long journey. He picked up his mobile phone and read the message again, 'Be careful not to stand in our way or we will deal with you soon!'An anonymous number had texted him during the day.

He got out of bed and monitored TV and radio stations for updates on the escalating violence. It happened that Luscano had triggered the clashes with inciting comments made on his radio programme. Luscano was 'a loose cannon' in Masem media as his platform became a forum for waging unprovoked wars of words against perceived political adversaries. Speculative analysis and conspiracy theories characterised his shows as he daily churned out alarming and damning utterances that fell out of sync with any of decorum and professional journalism. Through media mischief and sustained disparaging campaigns, Luscano engineered great disaffection within the populace and Masem was at a tipping point of chaos.

Whose agenda was Luscano pushing with this brand of journalism? Was it commercial interest that determined the content of his programme or political advantage that called the shots? Susubribi contemplated these questions and recalled that Luscano, Propgantus and Radicus were profiled by the *Discerning Minds Magazine*, spotlighting their crude activities in media and politics. Luscano used his platform to push the agenda of his political allies; Radicus and Propgantus and persistently waged subtle ethno-political warfare against their opponents.

The diagnostic findings by the magazine established that people who engaged in ethnic or hate politics often suffered from inferiority complex and needed to be reoriented to embrace their human dignity. It was unwise to feel inferior or superior to any ethnic group, tribe or race since the value of the human person was not based on one's acquired or ascribed identity but his humanity. Luscano and his friends suffered from a low self-esteem that found expression in highly pronounced prejudice. They could hardly engage their political opponents in issues-based discourse without personal attacks or whipping up tribal sentiments.

Susubribi hurriedly got up and went to his library to refresh his memory with the report. It was titled;'Falling Standards in Today's Journalism and Political Communication.' The report decried growing levels of intemperate language in media and public discourse and challenged stakeholders to help raise the bar. The forward-looking media and political analyst who authored the report warned of troubling times if the likes of Luscano, Propgantus and Radicus in media and politics were not called to order. There were reactionary attempts to sanitise the airwaves and ensure decency in discourse when the report was published but relevant stakeholders reneged and settled for the status quo.

Failure of relevant institutions to apply strict sanctions in respect of such violations accounted for the upsurge of derogatory contents and aggressive political communication in Masem media. This exposed citizens to scary cycles of violence and tensions. Many were left wondering what propelled the ambitions of those political actors and media professionals who continued to toy with the peace of the nation.

The concerns raised by the analyst seemed to be playing out in detail. Susubribi began to think deeply after reading the report for the second time. He was not going to mince words at the next leadership meeting. As the communications of the IP, he resolved to embark on a relentless campaign to ensure that healthy discourse prevailed over personal attacks and insults. Leaders who fell short of issues-based discourse and engaged in insulting, divisive and inciting remarks were to be sanctioned to serve as a deterrent to all members of the party.

CHAPTER TWO

'I cannot understand why some people begin so well but end up disappointing everyone,' an old man lamented. He was standing in front of his house where a group of people had gathered discussing the raging violence.

'When Luscano first appeared on radio,' he continued, 'many of us held the view that his fidelity to the national cause was above any selfish motivation. Regrettably, it is now certain his initial stance was only a smokescreen to hoodwink admirers. He has become a hate-monger, who finds interest in dredging up ethnic sentiments and fanning divisive politics. Look at the trouble he has caused,' the old man fumed.

'You are on point old man. It appears he also has an agenda to slander and ridicule some eminent figures in Masem. Those who have monitored him for a reasonable time can conclude he is bent on undermining leadership to promote a parochial interest,' a young man added.

'Do you admit that some of us are also part of the problem?' the old man asked.

'Why do you say so, oldie?' another person questioned.

'When Luscano was arrested a year ago for incitement,' he replied, 'we alleged his right to free speech was under attack and so we castigated the police until they bowed to pressure. We glossed over the seriousness of the offence and blindly alleged witch-hunting. In the chorus of unpatriotic confusion, he was left off the hook and continued beating war drums. Whenever we run to the defence of the lawless, we expose our lawless instincts and betray our resolve in promoting the rule of law. If we are not careful, the society will gradually wean itself off the oxygen (law) which infuses order. Without the citizens' unwavering support for law enforcement, society should expect the rule of the lawless and not the rule of law; chaos and not order,' the old man warned.

When a journalist becomes a hired man in the hands of sham politicians, destroying people becomes a source of livelihood sustained through nation-wrecking pronouncements. Luscano was on a mercenary path. He remained completely impervious to criticism and hailed the unpatriotic voices that showered flattering praises, blinding his conscience to what patriotic citizens saw as destructive journalism. 'Luscano, you are doing a great job,' some urged. 'We are solidly behind you my brother, continue the good work,' others encouraged. 'Fearless Luscano, keep up the bravado. Fire them! You are the man!' Some insisted.

In the heat of the mounting commotion, Luscano realized that freedom of the media, which he had religiously touted, was not absolute. There were laws in Masem to deal with errant elements that hid in the shadows of media freedom to perpetrate media terrorism. He slipped out of the city after a botched attempt by the police to pick him up. State security operatives and some politicians were suspected to have facilitated his escape and there was public backlash against officials believed to have done so. Such moles within the establishment derailed the fight against crime. Their allegiance to the state was blurred by sectional alliances which compromised patriotism. Luscano was declared wanted by the police but this move was ridiculed as lame because there was no point shutting the gate after the horse had bolted.

'No! This is getting serious! Look at the flames!' The alert saw the crowd fleeing the streets to escape the imminent danger of raging flames and rising smoke that consumed the building. The facility housed Masem Community Radio and other state installations but it was torched by some unrestrained members of the Politicus whose hearts were smouldering with violence.

The Politicus and Religis remained the two most dominant institutions that exerted enormous influence over the people of Masem. The Politicus, being the political class, competed among themselves for the mandate to determine Masem's policy direction. They were responsible for allocation of state power and resources and had to ensure that justice, equity and fairness prevailed. While some members of the Politicus were racking their brains for solutions to Masem's pressing challenges, others were actively engaged in unhealthy power struggle and primitive politicking. In their aggressive quest for power, they jeopardized national harmony by beating war drums, issuing threats, maligning well-meaning citizens, insulting and disrespecting notable persons.

Susubribi was a renowned member of the Politicus who continued to hold the torch of integrity in a political landscape that was being invaded by foul language, violence, corruption, dishonesty and greed. His mission in politics was motivated by a call to nation building and not for personal gain. He berated those who saw public office as an avenue for hoarding wealth to prop their egos and urged his colleagues to guard against plundering the public treasury. He often told his compatriots, 'If we fail to offer incorruptible service in the positions we find ourselves today, who will build the nation?' He was among the genuine ones who were passionate about the welfare of the people and inspired hope by giving meaning to what was possible; the politics of integrity.

The Religis in Masem professed deep knowledge about God and spirituality but there was a world of difference between what some of them propagated and what they practised. These ones sharply deviated from the cardinal tenets of their faith and were involved in the very things they openly denounced.

Divergent ideologies resulted in strained relations among sects and became a hotbed for unending conflicts. Some sects endorsed violent extremism and terrorized communities by arrogating unto themselves power to declare others unworthy of God's love and mercy. These developments were inspired by bitter intolerance as the search for God was confused with a desperate search for power, wealth and recognition. Accumulation of unmerited wealth became a great incentive for religious scammers who also invaded the realms of faith and paraded themselves as 'messengers of God' but they robbed even the poor to enrich themselves.

Masem was under siege by forces of corruption, dishonesty, greed, poverty and violence. The nation was in need of patriotic citizens to rescue the fate of generations. The Politicus and the Religis promised to offer leadership aimed at protecting the well-being of citizens and advancing the cause of the nation. However, people with disguised ambitions also crept into the corridors of power and lurked within the domains of faith but building the nation was not the mission inspired by their ambitions. Their conduct left much to be desired and so the question remained, who will build the nation?

CHAPTER THREE

Leaders of the IP were in a crunch meeting which saw high-powered officials arriving at the 17th Floor of the Awakening Heights. The mood was solemn, faces were serious and voices were subdued. Catching a glimpse through the windows, one was greeted with a striking vista of gleam and glamour. From here, one could satisfy the roving eyes by taking an unrestrained shot into the horizons where city lights appeared to be conversing with the dazzling stars of the skies. Judging the city of Masem by such looks of grandeur, one would have thought many of the people who lived here had escaped dire financial straits.

Ironically, beneath the splendour and sparkle which the city projected, many were still languishing in squalid deprivation. If the same aggression with which some politicians approached elections in Masem had been directed at confronting the challenges the people faced, significant progress would have been seen in the area of poverty eradication. Sadly, for some politicians in Masem, the threat of losing an election was more alarming than the challenges that plagued the electorate. This explains the pointless dissipation of great efforts and financial resources by certain individuals to wrestle power or hold on to it.

'On behalf of leadership, I welcome you to Awakening Heights. As leaders of the IP, we are significant players among the Politicus and so, we owe a non-negotiable duty to contribute to the security, peace and progress of this nation. All of us must be very careful to avoid instigating any action with a potential to ruin the nation we seek to build. If we mean well, we must rise against violence and expose the perpetrators in our midst. This evening, one question stands out. How do we end political violence in Masem? We must leave here, clear in our minds about how to assist the security agencies to rid our society of the errant ones who want to determine the political trajectory.

'If the right thinking ones in our midst will not resist deviance and show the way of acceptable conduct, then the corrupt and lawless ones in our fold will beat the insane path for us to follow. How can we build the nation if we become like them? Let us approach this discourse with the hope of charting a good course for all of our people. I humbly crave your indulgence to focus your contributions on the core agenda for this evening. Thank you,' the Chairman of the IP said.

The hall was sparsely crowded when the meeting formally opened but many leaders crammed the space within minutes and began making their contributions. After various submissions, Radicus asked to speak. He had a very intimidating presence because of his stature and when he stood up, all eyes were fixed on him. He twiddled with the microphone while waiting for the moderator to grant him permission.

'We can hear you now, Radicus,' the moderator announced.

'Comrades, last time, our opponents attacked one of our leaders on campaign but today they are at the receiving end. I understand their community leader is in critical condition. This is a clear case of retaliation in equal measure and as I have always maintained, tit for tat is fair play. They came with violence; we met them on their own terms and have beaten them to it. They must be told in clear terms that, they cannot stand us in the arena of violence. We must strategize to face them on any day! There are no friends on the other side of the divide! As for me, it is only elections I think about and that is my definition of political competition; organizing to win elections so you can wield power. Now, we must not fail to protect our guys because they have always fought for us to entrench our political fortunes. What is power if it cannot be exercised capriciously to serve your interests?' Radicus concluded.

'Well said, Radicus,' Propgantus gave him thumbs up. A unanimous silence greeted his proposal, but not all silence means consent as is often assumed. Leaders at the meeting were focused on one thing; ending political violence to guarantee security for all in Masem and not just for the elite. Trivializing a matter that had security implications would be a regrettable precedent that could open the floodgates for insecurity. They were certain and committed to fashioning out modalities to crush the incidence of militant activism in Masem.

Regrettably, Radicus and his camp thought their political fortunes depended on exerting coercion instead of negotiations, and that was what had made them relevant power brokers in the politics of Masem. Any attempt to clamp down on radical groups that had splintered off the IP, meant an end to their political mafia; an empire that had used brute force to hog undeserved recognition in Masem's political space.

'I beg to differ strongly with what Radicus has proposed,' Susubribi challenged. He continued, 'In the beguiling clutches of partisan extremism, foul play is often deemed as fair play but, we must hold our emotions in check for reason to present itself in any given contest or context. Our opponents are compatriots and more importantly, fellow humans who deserve love and respect, not hate and contempt. We must change the ugly face of politics for people to see the beauty of a healthy political competition. If we travel the path of vengeful rivalry, we will tear our nation apart, and how far can we go on the way of hatred and have our mutual peace and security? This is the

Party (IP) and so leadership must exhibit integrity to promote national cohesion and not rancour. Leaders who promote discord cannot be nation builders and the IP must rid itself of such individuals,' Susubribi said.

Many began casting glances at Radicus who had spoken earlier. They did not like his position on the matter but were afraid to openly voice out their views. It was as though Radicus was breathing down their necks. One was heard clearing his throat as if he was the one holding the microphone when Susubribi began to speak. He whispered into the ear of another, 'Susubribi has spoken my mind.'

'Yes, but I am afraid for him because he will become a target for Radicus. He is full of vindictiveness and will find a way to hit hard at him for dissenting,' he replied.

'Never mind, Susubribi is on a noble cause and no amount of intimidation or threats will make him change his position on this matter. He speaks his mind based on principle and will not recant based on fear. He will neither be captured by political correctness nor bow to the pressure of partisan malady. He is an iconic politician with an untainted political history and has remained one of the discordant voices in the chorus of political insanity. When one of our party communicators...aha I remember, it was Propgantus, when he went on radio and insulted leaders and members of the Religis, Susubribi was among the few who openly rebuked him. Susubribi is not a mainstream conformist who flows with the tide even when it is untidy and his exemplary disposition defies the claim that all politicians are the same. Let's listen, he is about to say more,' he said.

Susubribi sprang to his feet after the microphone had been fixed but he stopped because of a scratchy sound from the microphone. He sent a signal to the technicians to check the static feedback that reverberated through the hall. When the sound was normalised, he addressed the audience in remarks that left discerning minds looking for their thinking caps.

'As I speak, Masem is on the verge of explosion because of the unsettling menace of increasing radicalism. What has emboldened the activities of these political mercenaries? A year ago, ten people lost their lives to political violence in this city. Three months ago, a leading member of our party was a victim of mob assault, leading to his death. Today, it is a notable member of our opponents who is in critical condition. Whose fate is tied with the next violent attack?' he questioned.

'This is the moment for us to stamp our collective conscience on this hot-button issue. We cannot ignore sober reflection by playing to the gallery of folly. Any orientation towards extremism is inimical to a stable society and the vestiges of this warped culture within our body politic must not be allowed to flourish. Violent acts signal a threat to our collective security and if we are not careful, we will be creating a jungle society where those with rowdy inclinations shall dictate the pace of governance and leadership. We must never allow hoodlums to usurp the coercive powers of the state. We cannot sign a pact with insanity! No affiliation must guarantee a licence for lawless leaders and members of political groups to hold the rest of society to ransom.

'We face a grim prospect of gloomier days if we do not break any systemic shield protecting the cabal behind these crimes. On any day, it does not matter whose ox is gored, the law must take its course! It is high time people got to know that political parties are not safe havens for political rogues who think the party will always be there to defend their nefarious actions. It's a new day, it's a new dawn, and the party is no more a comfortable nest for predatory political birds. It will be to the detriment of us all if we continue pussyfooting at the brink of this abyss. We have to unite and act now! We must build the nation and not destroy it,' thank you.'

The applause was loud when Susubribi concluded but the remarks had ruffled the feathers of Radicus.

'We shall see...,' Radicus grumbled, and stormed out of the hall. All who heard him knew Susubribi was marked for a fist of fury.

CHAPTER FOUR

It was 2pm. Clouds of rain gathered in the skies over the city of Masem. Susubribi sat on his balcony and listened to country music as he overlooked the gardens in deep contemplation. *Dream Big* was the title of the song. The flowers in the yard were in a delightful dance to welcome the fresh wind blowing over the palatial residence. The birds dashed and perched from branch to branch as the trees swayed and waved from side to side in the gentle breeze. The dense canopy in the compound provided shade and restful warmth even on days when the sun gave blazing heat to households that had no trees. Susubribi had far exceeded the government's expectation in respect of its compulsory policy of at least one tree per household.

Looking down from the balcony, he saw a haggard looking woman heading towards his residence, with her baby strapped to her back. She limped slightly as she walked towards the gate with one slipper on her left foot and the other tucked under her armpit. She must have stumbled and torn the strap that fastened the slipper. She approached the security guard and pleaded with him for money to buy food. She turned to go when the security man was not able to help her but Susubribi called and asked her to be brought upstairs.

'How may I help you?' he asked but she appeared reticent for a moment. She and her husband had been hit by hard times and were struggling to find their faltering feet in life. Her husband lost his job about a year ago and had been grappling with mounting debts. Frantic efforts made to pull themselves from financial distress had hit a snag. They were really strapped for cash in a city where life without money was like travelling on a desert without water. Her husband went out for a menial job at a construction site and was wounded in the head by a falling block. He has been at home for weeks and she has also stopped petty trading because their baby was barely a month old. They had run out of cash and so she mustered courage and stepped out to see if someone could help them buy food for the day.

Susubribi entered his room and returned with an envelope stuffed with cash and gave it to her.

'Use some of the money for his medical care and come with him when he recovers. I will share an experience which may be helpful to you,' he assured her.

One afternoon, the couple came to Susubribi to thank him for the financial support and to listen to what he had promised to share with them.

'What makes you look so down and uninspired by any prospects in life?' Susubribi asked the man whose face bore marks of anxiety and despair.

'How can a man stay without worrying when he

is swallowed in debts that continue to eat away all his gains? I long for financial independence so that I can meet the basic demands of life. I have made several efforts but financial success seems to escape my chase,' he replied.

'I see the challenge but you shall overcome if your efforts do not waver,' Susubribi encouraged him.

'Yes, I know but I blame it all on some relations. If I had gotten support from them, I would not have been struggling today. Honestly, I am very bitter about their treatment,' he lamented. Susubribi listened as he sipped some wine. He placed the glass on the table and looked intently at his guests, in whose faces he could read signs of dejection.

'O why are you bitter?' Susubribi asked.

'Hmm,' the man sighed and replied, 'Sometimes, I miss the innocence of childhood when goodness ruled my heart. I had no grudges. I nurtured no ill-feelings and desired to hurt no one. I was kind, forgiving, compassionate and loving. Those were the days when peace and harmony ruled my world. But as I travelled through the years and became an adult; faced with the responsibilities and challenges of the real world, I learned to be unkind, bitter and unforgiving to the point of being cruel sometimes. I am not at peace with myself because I am not able to forgive them,' he opened up.

'Hmmm... your words have evoked great memo-

ries of my childhood. My mother told me to bemoan my inability to help others and not the inability of others to help me. Think this way and you will be free from bitterness which is a great saboteur to self-development. Those words have healed many souls. Mother was right! May her soul, rest in peace. Tell me, how long can you remain bitter and live with worry? Worriers die young so, stop fretting and free your mind of any burden. Life presents us with numerous challenges as well as endless opportunities but if you remain handcuffed by your challenges, you cannot stretch out your hands for any opportunity,' Susubribi counselled him.

'Note this, in any endeavour, one's background does not rule out the possibility of success or failure. In the matrix of progress, effort cannot be discounted from the equation of desire and focus,' Susubribi remarked. He placed two more bottles of wine on the table for his guests after the first one had been emptied.

'Based on my social standing, some people I have met think I have not known suffering. We only marvel at the magnificence of a mansion and often forget to acknowledge the toil and sweat of the poor labourers whose breaking backs laid the foundation for the imposing edifice to stand. I have been at the bottom of deep financial crisis and I sunk so low that rising seemed impossible,' Susubribi narrated. 'This nearly crushed my resolve,' he continued, 'but I kept the focus and looked into the future with great expectation. Trust me, I have tasted poverty and I have tasted wealth. I have failed in one thing and succeeded in another. I am always thankful for the guiding principles my parents shared with me. These solid values have shaped my life and made me a better person. You don't have to let your pain make you bitter because that can lead you on the path of regrettable crimes. Let your pain become the catalyst for the demonstration of your strength, not your weakness, your wisdom and not your folly,' Susubribi philosophized.

'Thank you very much! This is an eye-opener,' the man commended.

'Yes, deeply enlightening,' his wife added.

'Now, listen carefully to what I am about to share with you and you will take full responsibility of your life without blaming anyone for your state,' Susubribi told them. 'Some scenes....' he was about sharing his story when the phone rang. He excused his guests and attended to the call.

CHAPTER FIVE

'Some scenes from childhood are always present in my memory,' Susubribi continued after the call. 'One night, my mother got up to reposition some of our belongings in the room in order to prevent them from being drenched by rainwater. The downpour had lasted for barely half an hour but the leakages had almost filled to the brim the bowls she placed to collect the drops. Barimah; my father was in a deep slumber after a hard day's labour. He slept and snored as the rains poured heavily on his roof. He would have awakened to find himself swimming in a pool in his own room if Obaa had not tapped him on the back. He squinted as he looked at the flickering lantern.

"Is it raining?" he asked.

"Yes" Obaa replied.

'Barimah got up and threw his cloth over his shoulders. He picked up the lantern and raised it up to check the leakages. He had climbed the roof a month ago to seal the holes but new ones had developed and needed to be patched. Obaa mopped the floor with rags and collected the bowls to throw the water away but she slipped and fell down, slightly spraining her spine. She shivered in the cold weather and hoped the rains would subside so she could lay the mat again and have some rest. Holding on to the wings of hope was a daily habit that prevented her from falling down into the pit of desperation. The journey was gruelling but she stood the chequered times with Barimah through it all and never lost hope in the man she saw in him. She valued his worth over his wealth and father was aiming to share a great future with the woman who shared his aspirations. He would often tell his friends, "She is my Jew, like a jewel; more precious than the prized pearls of Sheba."

'Obaa woke up in the morning with a feeling of intense pain in her back. She staggered towards the door and supported herself on a stool as her wobbling legs could no longer stand. Barimah massaged her back with boiled water to soothe the pain but she showed no sign of improvement. Our neighbours who visited urged her to go to hospital for treatment but she knew the hospital was not a place for all who were ill but those who could afford it. Barimah combed through the village for a loan to take Obaa to the hospital but was still unsuccessful. The next day, he left home early morning and walked from one place to the other with the hope of securing a loan.

After hours of trekking, he sat under a tree near Sika's house to take some minutes rest from the scorching sun. He had neither eaten nor drank and appeared physically frazzled and emotionally drained. He wiped his forehead with his finger to reduce the beads of sweat that trickled down his face. He stared at Sika's compound and saw the children playing gaily inside the yard. Sika would have lent him any amount upon request if he had gone to him but he shrugged off the thought. He had decided not to borrow money again from a man who had subjected him to such a degree of humiliation. That was last month when he defaulted. Going back to Sika will mean he had suppressed his dignity but what value was there in a man's dignity for him to protect when the life of his wife was on the line? He had always insisted that saving one's integrity should supersede dignity whenever one was torn between the two considerations. He felt telling his ears "Barimah, your pride can be your plight."

'When he delayed in returning home, some neighbours decided to take Obaa to the hospital because her condition had deteriorated. A feeling of nausea and dizziness seized her and she quivered when they held her. She looked pale and feeble and needed to be admitted but she had no money to even attract a doctor's attention. They lingered helplessly at the hospital, being turned away at every point because they could not pay. Finally, she tumbled down the stairs. They grabbed her frail body and shouted for help but the hospital authorities denied any assistance.

'Minutes later, Barimah bumped into the hall sweating profusely. He wore a dejected look and appeared as helpless as a chicken escaping a thunderstorm. The little confidence in him had waned and the dust gathered on his feet showed he had walked miles. Sika had given him a loan and he was ready to pay for medical care only to be told that Obaa had yielded to the bitter caress of lasting sleep. "O she is dead," he was told. They ushered him into a room and found her body cuddled in the unpleasant bosom of a shroud. He could not bear to stare beyond her plated hair. Torrents of tears rolled down his eyes as he moved out of the room.

"Ah! How darkness falls at noonday! The sun is shining but my day is darkened! I never knew there could be this darkness at noon," he cried. More questions invaded his thoughts but accurate answers eluded his mind. "O poverty, why do you hate prosperity?" he grieved.

'A year later, Barimah had also joined the mortal train. At age 16, I had lost both parents but the key lessons they shared later shaped my focus in life and influenced my progress. Before his demise, Barimah told me, "Susubribi, your name will ring a bell in the halls of inspiration if you aspire for what brings meaning to humanity. You must take risks in order to reach your dreams but that should not stop you from thinking through your decisions and considering contingencies before embarking on any venture. If you do this, you will scale many hurdles and avoid pitfalls.

'I desired financial freedom and so I set out to invest in numerous businesses to guarantee multiple streams of income. When my appetite for huge profits had grown, I was introduced to a business that promised exponential returns. In spite of the high risk hovering around the enterprise, I ventured with eagerness and made a huge investment. In my estimation, I was on a streak of fortune and felt this was time to make it big and pursue other shelved ambitions. It was nerve-wracking when I came to know that my investment had gone down the drain. My indiscretion led me down this path of great financial difficulty and I have since been clutching at straws to regain a lost fortune. I never contemplated that my greed could bleed into such an alarming loss.

"My son, aim at higher heights but never allow your thirst for success, overcome your quest for fairness and moderation. Create space for the needs of others and not just your own." My father shared this insight. I will continue the story after you have eaten,' Susubribi paused and ordered food for his guests.

CHAPTER SIX

Susubribi resumed the narration after feeding his guests, 'I witnessed the back-breaking drudgery my parents had to endure in the village. But for the benevolence of generous hearts that came to our rescue in moments of difficulty, there were times we could have died destitutes. It was a life of constant struggle and hustle in a community where poverty was a companion of the masses but wealth, a friend of the few.

'Dire poverty strained the energies of poor parents and ravaged the fertile minds of their children. I and my siblings shared similar fate with other children in the village. We wore tattered clothing. We walked miles to school bare foot. We dropped out of schools because our peasant parents could hardly pay our fees. We engaged in laborious works. We suffered the pangs of starvation. Some died of curable diseases. Great talents got buried unutilized.

'Without adequate financial security, we were exposed to the perils of life like birds without feathers. It was pain and misery!

'Surrendering to join the masses jostling at the bottom of the social pile appeared the easy way that would have relieved me of the strenuous challenges. But I needed to do something about the sorry narrative. I needed to lay building blocks for a meaningful life. I had to surmount the obstacles and not allow setbacks to spell a dead end to my aspirations. In order to succeed, I had to shoot through barriers with a determined spirit and laser-focus. Friends told me to open my eyes so I can see clearly, but father had said, "Son, open your mind always, so you can see afar."

'I broadened my scope and began exploring more opportunities in pursuit of the dream; the prospect of making a positive impact on society. I experienced a new lease of life the moment I changed lanes from wishful thinking to purposeful action. I skimped and saved my meagre earnings to pursue higher learning. Through grit, I became an accomplished lawyer and rose through the ranks to become an influential member of the Politicus.

'Now, I have given a gist of how I had to roll with the punches life threw at me in order to reach my desired destination. I was poised for a change and had to bargain with circumstances to make it possible. I knew there was something to gain on the road of pain than the illusory comfort convenience always gave.

'Barimah had told me, "When man plays his part and extenuating circumstances outplay his efforts, there should be no despair. However, if he sits aloof and only whines, he shall suffer the reproach of inaction." A lazy person, he said, is not a victim of poverty but the architect of it. Such inspiring words spurred me on even in the face of frustrating adversities.

'Whenever I was bogged down by hard blows of life and felt like giving up or settling for the ease of complacency, I was nudged into action by the echoing call constantly summoning me to my life's duty; a personal contribution to humanity. I am still pushing the limits not just for myself, but for those destiny requires I offer social support.

'My humble background and the circumstances of my upbringing have imbued in me a great sense of sensitivity to the plight of the downtrodden. I cannot forget that while some of us are cooling off within the confines of wealth and pleasure, others are languishing in penury and pain. I will help you to escape poverty but never forget; others would be enduring that which you have escaped. We must show gratitude to our Creator by easing the harrowing pains of the poor and vulnerable in our societies through charities. If this continues, together, we shall all make a difference.

' As an entrepreneur, I know wealth can do a lot of good. So I tell people, let's think of wealth creation. Let's think of poverty eradication. Let's innovate and generate great ideas that transform lives. Let's establish legitimate businesses and rake in honest profits so we can always promote the social good. We who are wealthy are stewards with a mandate to expend our resources in the supreme interest of humanity, especially, those in

Mind you, one man's selfishness can leave many in the grips of poverty just as a selfless act of an individual can usher many into the domain of prosperity,' Susubribi concluded.

His desire to see many families cross the poverty line made him instrumental in ensuring children in Masem had free access to school. He knew this was one of the surest ways to evacuate generations from the trenches of poverty. Poor families that hitherto could not send their children to school were now relieved of the burden that came with funding. He advocated the rolling out of more of such all-inclusive programmes to ease the financial strain on communities that bore the brunt of marginalization.

His recent visit to the hinterlands revealed that more families were still grappling with hard labour, hunger and ill health. His heightened social conscience made him very passionate about the wellbeing of the nation and not the perks that came with the position. He was focused on working to alleviate the plight of generations and not obsessed with the trivial triumph of elections. Susubribi was a real politician and not a sham, a nation builder and not a political opportunist.

The couple arrived home and began brainstorming business ideas. Susubribi had told them to decide on a lucrative venture that had the potential to transform their lives. He was ready to assist them with start-up capital. 'I will help you to escape poverty. Present your business plan to me by tomorrow so you can get started,' he had assured them.

They wanted to put the baby to sleep and continue planning but the baby continued to cry.

'It could be an illness,' his wife said.

'I thought as much. I will go out and get medicine for him,' he told her and stepped out into the dark and empty street. The baby's cry cut through his ear and made him run as fast as he could. He was quick to get to the pharmacy shop but it was closed. He knocked and called but no one answered.

'What are you looking for?' Someone bellowed from behind him. He turned to look but he was dazed by a stone that was hurled at him in the chest.

'Thief! Thief!' Two stout young men gripped him by the waist of his trouser while alarming residents. He broke off their hold and ran but they ran after him shouting,

'Thief! Thief!'

'No! I'm not a thief. I was here to buy medicine,' he cried but his assailants would not listen.

'You are a liar! Who goes out to buy medicine at this hour?' One of them replied as he chased him. He jumped over a gutter and was nearly out of their sight but fell over a block and landed flat on the chest. Another stone whizzed past his ears and hit the ground. He got up to run but one person pounced on him in cruel brutality and struggled to get a firm hold of him. He wriggled free of his embrace and escaped but they pursued him with even greater fury, growling, 'Arrest and lynch him!' Turning back, he saw a much thicker mob than he had seen a moment ago running after him but he dashed into a nearby bush and sneaked behind a bushy mound.

'He passed here!'Someone directed, pointing his stick at his hiding place but the lynch mob ran past the spot shouting, 'Chase him! He is a thief!' He crept backwards and went under the greens as a few of them trudged through the bushes on an aggressive hunt. He crawled to hide in a trench overgrown with weeds and stayed still to avoid being noticed.

'I said he passed here! Look into the bushes!' The one in front insisted as he climbed up the mound and looked around in all directions. Hey! He is here! Come over! He rolled down the mound and swooped on him violently. He grabbed him by the neck but he wrestled with him until they ended up in a clinch.

'Come quickly. He wants to run again!' He lost strength and gave up fighting for his life as they clobbered him with sticks and pelted him with stones. He was overpowered and dragged to the open where his body became a beehive for a swarming mob of irate neighbours.

'Pl-ea-se t-a-ke me to the po-li-ce... I –am- not- a

–thief.' He struggled to speak but kindness had fled from the hearts of the mob. He was battered and tortured with any object they could find. Even in his dying voice, he continued to utter a plea but his cry for mercy was ignored by the instincts of vicious madness. His body was left sprawling on the ground; lynched to death in a horrifying fashion of man's inhumanity to his fellow human.

'No! This is not the way to go!! We cannot build a nation with this inhuman cruelty!!! O my people, we are humans so let's be humane!!!' One person protested the sheer callousness but he was shoved aside and told, 'Do not pity a thief!' His lone voice of reason was unable to stand the unconscionable anger that poured out of their hearts.

Without recourse to the law, they committed a grievous crime but claimed they were fighting crime. The ugly canker of mob injustice seemed ingrained in the social fabric of a section of the Masem society which remained unrepentant and continued to tolerate lynching in various communities. Calls for drastic action to bury this obnoxious practice in the dark history of the past, remained unheard as families continued to wail for their loved ones who fell victim to the gruesome practice. Leaders of Masem were yet to put a firm foot on the ground to give meaning to the law that prohibited lynching.

CHAPTER SEVEN

The Sage of Masem was a respected leader and truce broker who strove for peace in the land. It was said he had engaged with ancient texts and gleaned insight buried in pages few cared to open. He had also sat at the feet of the sages and drank beads of wisdom dripping from white beards. Probity and wisdom made the old man a towering force to reckon with in the battle of minds. One of his greatest concerns was to see Masem rid itself of the culture of violence and antagonism that continued to threaten the harmonious progress of the nation.

On the greenery hills of Masem perched the time-honoured cottage of the Sage. The far-flung countryside was an intellectual home to great leaders as it served as a citadel of enlightenment to those willing to broaden their perspectives on leadership. Here, leaders converged to critically reason in order to find solutions to the myriad challenges in their communities. This explains why the place was so named; Reasoning Hills. Those who came here found themselves in the soothing embrace of a rejuvenating quietude offered by the fresh air that blew from the giant trees of the salubrious forest. It was breath-taking to hear the birds singing in the sweet melody of nature's serenity. The city's incessant noise had fainted in the dying echoes of consciousness.

Climbing up the hill, one was greeted with an imposing signboard and the visible inscription was to remind citizens of Masem to preserve the gift of nature and stop environmental degradation.

THE NATION YEARNS, THE NATION WAILS
IN THE DISTANCE OF TIME, THE NATION MOANS
BECAUSE OF HER DESTROYERS
IN THE MIDST OF ABUNDANCE YOU HAVE CREATED SCARCITY
ON THE SHORES OF WEALTH YOU HAVE HEWN POVERTY
YOU BROWN THE GREENS OF NATURE
ONLY TO DRY YOURSELVES IN THE SCORCHING RAYS OF DANGER
YOU ARE SEARED IN THE PARCHING WOES OF DEGRADATION
INSTEAD OF COOLING OFF IN THE DENSE WOODS OF THE VEGETATION
WHY QUENCH YOUR THIRST WITH DROPS
INSTEAD OF BEING REFRESHED WITH
SPLASHING SPARKLING WATER SWIRLING
FROM ROCKY MOUNTAINS OF THE GREEN FORESTS?
WHO WILL LET THE TREES GROW?
WHO WILL LET THE RIVERS FLOW?
WHO WILL RECLAIM THE LAND?
WHO WILL BUILD THE NATION?

At 10:45am, the hall was almost full but some were still thronging the upper chamber to find seats. The boisterous hall gave way to calmness when the Sage finally reached the dais. He yielded to a noticeable stoop, a telling indication that the old man had wrestled with time and age. They stood up and recited the nation builders' pledge,

"I shall not be a party to any cause that promotes sectional interest against the national good;
I shall promote the rule of law and be law abiding,
I shall denounce violence and will not subscribe to any violent activity,
I shall detest, expose and report crime or corrupt activities to appropriate authorities,
I shall diligently offer constructive contribution towards nation building, by remaining true to my conscience and integrity,
I will not sow seeds of discord or cause disaffection within the society,
I will not insult, defame or denigrate anyone because;
I have a nation to build and a great future to bequeath to posterity."

'You are once again welcome to Reasoning Hills,' in a soft but clear voice, the Sage greeted. He walked to the right side of the podium and placed the walking stick close to his seat. 'As you are aware, at Reasoning Hills, we gather not to chatter but to critically think and reason. We ask stimulating questions and broach topics that are relevant to nation building. At Reasoning Hills, we ignite a bolstering force for continuous debates and dialogues aimed at combating societal nightmares for a peaceful and orderly society. This has been the long-standing tradition, defining our mission. Our role in nation building is not limited to the positions we aspire or the ones we occupy wherever we find ourselves, we can make a difference. The clock is ticking, duty is calling, generations are expecting, who will build the nation?' the Sage charged.

The engrossing lecture in the first session left the audience yearning for more and at 2pm, they returned to the hall to enjoy more insightful conversations and thought-racking expositions from the Sage.

'Be minded of the ground rules and focus on issues and not personalities. I have often told you, *ad hominem*(personal attack) is barred from Reasoning Hills. In the contest of minds, those bereft of ideas seek refuge in personal attacks but great minds have risen above obscenity by consciously refining their language,' the Sage advised. 'Now, you can ask your questions,' he informed as several hands went up.

'Ok, you,' he pointed at a man in the front row, wearing a white shirt. He was one of the leading journalists in Masem known for honesty and integrity in his professional conduct.

'Great Sage, I salute you for this national assignment. You have always charged us to be active players in nation building and not cynical bystanders who only whine. You have said we should not compromise our civic responsibilities for extremely partisan activities. Your wise counsel has guided many political actors to become nation builders but there are some who continue to muddy the political waters and make mockery of political competitions in Masem. Tensions and contentions continue to dominate the discourse even as parties scramble to lead the nation. This has created flashpoints that require heavy security presence during elections.

'Even after elections, political rivalry continues to obstruct national cohesion and hinders the collective goodwill needed in building the nation. It appears those in power are regarded by majority of the opposition as imperialists who deserve no goodwill no matter the good they do. Members of the opposition are seen by most members of government as traitors deserving to be kept at the fringes of decision making irrespective of their good intentions. We seem to have accepted the unfortunate development as a permanent feature of our political culture and so the aggression keeps growing and the division keeps widening.

'We desire to see constructive cooperation instead of excessive confrontation in the nation's communicators, what should be our approach to media and political communication so as to engineer national cohesion and not polarisation?' The respected journalist asked.

'This is a very important question. It is no wonder that you are a distinguished media personality. You have always put the interest of the nation above any other consideration. I will answer your question in a moment,' the Sage paused to drink water.

CHAPTER EIGHT

Misinformation is a threat to the progress of any society. It is regrettable how some have gained notoriety for allowing anything to be strewn over the airwaves without recourse to best journalistic practices. It appears people are wilfully uninformed about the fact that certain matters do not belong to certain quarters. Why rush to the media with very sensitive issues that have dire consequences to security or reputations?' the Sage asked.

'We have heard of the infamous Luscano but what lessons have we learnt? Luscano typifies destructive journalism and reckless political communication that erode national cohesion. After reviewing his case, we should be abreast of the right approach to political communication so as to foster development in harmony. Nation builders must study this case and be wary of the blunders that mire and mar constructive discourse,' the Sage informed.

'Luscano triggered a mob attack on a leading figure of the Politicus a few weeks ago. A party communicator went on his radio programme and claimed there were shady attempts by leaders of the IP to rig the forthcoming elections in Masem. He made several unsubstantiated allegations and fanned ethnic sentiments with the tacit support of Luscano. Typical of Luscano's self-styled journalism, he also incited the public through misleading narratives. Other media houses picked up the story and reported without fact-checking those claims. A group of unidentified men acted on these claims and attacked a leading political figure. Masem was thrown into a state of insecurity and the city was placed on lockdown for a whole day. Events occur and there are lessons in their trail for us to learn. It appears some of us have not learnt vital lessons from the Luscano debacle and are daily repeating the very mistakes that disturbed our peace.

'The media must beware; sometimes, in our hurry to break the news, we break hearts, sometimes, in our zeal to gain considerable attention or traction, we cause irreparable destruction. We must not sell stories to compromise our security or undermine our sovereignty. Great citizens display thoughtfulness and high levels of responsibility in their media engagements. Responsible citizens are peacemakers and not war-mongers; they offer constructive criticisms and do not engineer destructive cynicism. Media houses must reject those who consistently display unruly emotions on their platforms. Journalists must exercise proactive discretionary censorship (PDC) to disallow fighting words, insults and a call to violence.

'Those who lack civility cannot command decency in public discourse and do not have what it takes to be at the forefront of communication. Owners and managers of media houses must not allow loose cannons in communication to run programmes or even appear as panellists on their platforms if they are mindful of the national interest. When we are proactive in this regard, we will mitigate polarisation and prevent a lot of conflicts waiting to explode as a result of irresponsible communication,' the Sage warned.

'Please, sometimes we play the devil's advocate by stoking flames of controversy or fuelling the rumour mill. How does that play out in the scheme of things?' another journalist asked.

'Don't be the devil's advocate but be the opponent's advocate. Employ 'strategic opposition' as I call it, to excite fruitful conversations or highlight opposing viewpoints but that should not be confused with advocating orchestrated allegations and bandying conceited opinions as facts. To stand out as a journalist or a political communicator who promotes unity, one should resist the temptation of professional tale bearing and focus on issues that advance nation building. Our job must not make us conduits for calumny but seekers of truth and advocates of public welfare.

'Journalism is not about snooping into the personal affairs of citizens or prying into the private lives of public figures as some have made it. In the hands of honest citizens, journalism is a great tool for driving positive social change and fostering national cohesion. However, when professional mercenaries parade the airwaves or write the pages, journalism loses its nobility as dishonesty, mudslinging, hate language, blackmail and bewildering effusions become the norm.

'A nation is threatened when progressive journalism is under siege from ego-trippers and mercenaries who promote their own agenda. Political parties and managers of media houses must have people with integrity at the forefront of communication to drive the national discourse beyond the crudities of professional charade.

'To promote national cohesion, Masem does not need emotional amateurs who excite the airwaves with tantrums and unrestrained antics. We need mature communicators who elevate the debate by offering constructive arguments and consciously considering the broader national interest and not those with insidious agenda to engineer hatred and attack personalities. Prominence must be shifted from those caught in the web of crass propaganda, uncouthness, and insensitive political point scoring,' the Sage averred.

'People who cannot run with the H-O-R-S-E or fly with the E-A-G-L-E will never have their place at the table of prominence when the roll of patriotic citizens is called. Running with the H-O-R-S-E means being Honest, Objective, Respectful,

Sensitive and Ethical in your appreciation and presentation of issues at all times. Flying with the E-A-G-L-E also means being Ethical, Accurate, Genuine, Level-headed and Equitable at all times. I mean at all times. Those without grounding in the H-O-R-S-E or E-A-G-L-E principles shall suffer the resentment of generational scrutiny.

'A little massaging of facts, a little spinning of information and a man's verdict is crystallized in the records of society. Let's be careful we do not earn public certification for mendacity. We lose our relevance in national discourse when credibility deficit is scored. Those who peddle lies and churn out blatant propaganda hinged on overt or covert agenda to run down individuals and institutions do not build but destroy the nation.

'In our stock taking, such disrespectful and dishonest citizens shall always be regarded as traitors of the common good. We do our nation great disservice if we allow people like that become the mouthpieces and torchbearers of our national discourse,' the Sage said, shedding more light on the subject.

'Comrades of media and politics, you owe a duty to society. What you say, what you write, shall not escape the scrutiny of posterity. Fan not the sentiments that divide us and fray not the bonds that bind us, or else, we will fall apart! Build your nation but don't destroy it.'

Many of the participants were seen busily

jotting down notes even as the sage left the stage with unending applause from the audience.

CHAPTER NINE

'Ask your questions,' the Sage told the audience after the break. A lady got up and began, 'Great Sage, I am an active politician and I admit that Masem is faced with the challenge of adversarial politics. The incessant display of paranoia especially, during elections is an affront to our forward march. It has been difficult achieving national cohesion because the polarity of our political leadership is more telling than its solidarity.

'Unhealthy aggression continues to pose serious threat to what ought to be our collective resolve; fighting crime and poverty. Many politicians need to change course from the present terrain of scandalous bad faith, excessive suspicion and unreasonable mistrust. Please what should we do to promote healthy political competitions in Masem?

'That's a great question,' the Sage commended. 'The maturity of any democracy is determined by the constructiveness of its opposition and inclusiveness of its government. How do we work together to find accessible and affordable healthcare and education to majority of our people? How do we work together to evacuate majority of our people from the trenches of poverty and provide them with decent standard of living? These are critical matters that should always engage the minds of leaders of political parties and not the endless election-related bickering. How long are we going to entertain dirty politics at the expense of nation building?

'Political leaders must constantly reposition themselves for the good of the nation because we cannot build together when we keep standing apart on pertinent national issues. In an atmosphere of excessive suspicion and ill-will, there cannot be a healthy partnership for accelerated development. We can change that trend when we rise above antagonism and bury virulent communication. When there is too much confrontation and rancour instead of cooperation and rapport, a nation suffers stunted progress. There is no time in the future than now for patriotism to override blind partisan activism.

'Leadership must be a social vehicle; constantly carrying the people on the path of consensus and cohesion and not that of confusion and division. To do this, political parties must meticulously put efficient systems in place to eliminate political rogues from party hierarchy. They must look within to purge themselves of leaders whose conduct and utterances promote strife.

'A nation is undermined when traitors of the rule of law infiltrate the ranks of political leadership. History shall forever frown at their memory with great rage and indignity for being proponents of troubling confusion and not promoters of national cohesion. If we sit at the table of reason, we cannot allow ideological differences to drown our common humanity in the well of animosity. There is no wisdom in fighting among ourselves when we can join hands to fight poverty and crime threatening our communities.

'We can cede more of our partisan political turfs and bend towards negotiations for unimpeded harmony and progress. We can sound persuasive and conciliatory to those with dissenting views than being abrasive and combative. We can show magnanimity even in criticism and avoid blistering attacks on those with differing opinion. We would be marching on the path of peace and cohesion for progress and prosperity if we can work as partners in nation building and not adversaries,' the Sage admonished the audience.

'Respected Sage, I have heard people say, politics is a dirty game. Others have also claimed that all politicians are the same. By this, they mean, all politicians are corrupt, dishonest and insensitive to the needs of the masses. Even some journalists in Masem who are supposed to inform and educate their audience rather misinform and mislead the public by reinforcing this saint-playing fallacy. Often, those of us who are not into active politics lump all politicians and tag them negatively as if all politicians do not mean well for the nation. Are all politicians the same, as claimed and is politics a dirty game?' a gentleman asked.

'OK, let us exercise informed judgement devoid

of bias in this matter,' the sage requested. 'Respond yes or no after each of the following statements,' he demanded.

'All journalists are the same.'

'No!' the audience exclaimed.

'All lawyers are the same.'

'No!'

'All judges are the same.'

'No!'

'All doctors are the same.'

'No!'

'All bankers are the same.'

'No!'

'All lecturers are the same.'

'No!'

'All students are the same.'

'No!'

All civil society organisations are the same?

'No!'

'All religions are the same.'

'No!'

'All religious people are the same.'

'No!'

'All political parties are the same.'

'No!'

'All politicians are the same.'

'No!'

'You have given a fair verdict and I share in that considered opinion. It is extremely inconsiderate to represent the whole with the bad nut. Yes, I admit, there are sham politicians but, all politicians are not sham. It flies in the face of critical thinking to assume that all politicians are the same. This overblown generalization has become a licensed stereotype that continues to engineer mass prejudice against politicians and it must not be encouraged.

'Politics is not a dirty game. It is some political players who play dirty games in politics. Politics is a legitimate enterprise and there are many decent and patriotic politicians who are passionately working to build the nation. Let's not ungratefully douse the positive energies of selfless politicians, who are passionately contributing their part to nation building,' the Sage advised them.

CHAPTER TEN

'Thank you for the education, learned Sage. From the little I have studied from the history of Masem, I am tempted to say, religion and politics have occasioned most of our dark moments than any other social institution. Cruel conflicts and wild wars have been fought in the name of politics or religion. Rivers of blood have been spilled throughout the land for power and for faith. As I speak, Masem is not calm because of sporadic tensions which are religiously and politically motivated. Now, this is my question; power and faith, do they pose existential threat to humanity or promise to safeguard our collective survival? Will they be the key drivers of global disorder or harmony, misery or triumph?' a diplomat wanted to know.

'As leaders of today and tomorrow, these questions should grab our consciousness,' the Sage observed. 'Looking at the horrible excesses, should we even detest religion or politics or both? No, not religion but religious extremism. Not politics, but political fanaticism. Religion and politics are the two legs with which nations have walked their journeys through life but politics without integrity is like religion without spirituality; they remain decadent, corrupt and retrogressive. It is this type that breed hatred, fraud, insecurity and horrifying crimes against humanity. When faced with one, we should not be afraid to ask critical questions that are likely to burst the bubble of those rusty dogmas or rattle the cage of such antiquated doctrines.

'The blazing torch of true enlightenment must crush the relics of false beliefs and monuments of bigotry etched on the minds of extremists. We must hone our minds to enlighten our world and save generations from phony concepts and theories that have darkened the world of fanatics. If we keep searching with an open mind, we can cross many ideological borders to embrace what is true and live by it. Falsehood is ephemeral but truth eternal,' the Sage underscored.

'The noble goal of religion must be to honour the Creator by serving humanity. The noble goal of politics must be to build the nation by serving its people. A lesser form of religion or politics is established if one's motivation for religion or politics deviates from these noble goals. Our common humanity means we owe ourselves eternal bonds of goodwill which religion and politics must strive to strengthen among people and not destroy.

'No identity can insulate any one of us from crimes that threaten humanity and our diversities must not serve as barriers impeding our collective resolve to confronting social ills. There is no cause greater than that which advances the cause of humanity and there is no evil greater than that which endorses crime against humanity,' the Sage added.

'Sir, this is *The Trends Newspaper.* The banner headline reads, "House of Representatives to Debate Same Sex Marriage." The crux of the story is that the House will soon be considering a proposal for the legislation of same sex marriage in Masem. I have always held the view that this matter should never be a subject for discussion because Masem is completely averse to homosexuality and cannot grant it social licence. My question is simple, how right is gay rights? Please where do you stand on this issue?' a gentleman asked.

'I stand on Reasoning Hills, but where do you also stand?' the sage replied in a jest that pleasantly excited the audience.

'Legalisation of homosexuality is legitimization of corruption; a blatant perversion of order,' the gentleman answered.

'Great! Subduing our inherent corruption is a task that propels growth and our ability to rise above the instincts of human decay is what elevates us above ordinary existence. Making laws to sanction our human foibles and frailties is a move that smacks of normalising abnormality and we should not be oblivious of the dire consequences,' the Sage cautioned. He continued,

'Some have argued that we live in an era of globalization and since the society is continually becoming a melting pot of diverse cultures and norms, we have got to be culturally permissive. I am a firm advocate of a progressive society and I embrace change for the good of humanity. I am also not ignorant of the dynamism of culture but I don't want to believe that globalization has come to dethrone our established norms and time-honoured values spanning across generations. We cannot shove aside our strong values which have been the bulwark against deviance and guaranteed our collective decency.

'Globalization has its own place in the social intercourse of trade, technology and international relations but it must not be a tool for negative indoctrination and assimilation. We cannot embrace lifestyles that can erode our moral architecture and crumble the very foundation of our social edifice. It is self-imposed tragedy, when a society unscrupulously grants licence to all manner of human cravings,' the Sage warned.

'Please what about human rights? Those who feel and wish to be gay must be gay and those who want to remain straight must remain straight. We must respect their fundamental human rights,' a human rights advocate insisted.

'Human rights...human rights...the often abused phrase. We cannot promote human rights and ignore human limitations,' the Sage observed. 'If all of our desires are deemed our rights, more rights would soon be our desire and the rights of all would be our utmost desire until our very humanity is threatened. Must the society cater to all of our desires?' He questioned. 'Unrestrained rights of all would be a threat to all. Without barriers in his way, man will be a god unto himself; religiously bowing to the dictates of his ravening desires and fleeting thoughts. It is only the fear of God that can make us upright humans who respect boundaries!

'To save our society from the path of peril, there must be reasonable limits to our base desires. If we acquiesce to our primordial instincts, we will fall prey to decadence and disorder. Same sex marriage is like an unguided arrow; it can break the moral code of generations. We have got to rethink our collective passivity and end the anomaly being worshipped on the altar of human rights. There are values that modernity must never attempt to negotiate; pillars we mustn't break!' the sage cautioned.

CHAPTER ELEVEN

'Great Sage, as a law student, my greatest concern is to see an era where we are able to block and re-channel the resources that continue to trickle down the tunnels of corruption year in and year out in Masem. Recent developments in the corporate world have exposed sophisticated fraud and organized crimes within institutions. Corrupt practices in the murky world of the Religis do not cause much sensation in society as that of the Politicus. Bribery involving members of the media often does not make headlines.

'Endemic corruption remains a daunting challenge to national progress. It will interest you to know that during campus elections, some of us try to circumvent due process for unfair advantage. We have learnt ways of getting around laid down procedures to grab whatever we desire irrespective of how costly it will be to other people. Some have graduated from school, joined mainstream politics or the world of work and are replicating this attitude in various institutions.

'Justice is earned by the deserving and must not be procured by the one with clout but there are some in the Judiciary who compromise than strive for and attain justice. Please, what is your perception of corruption and what corrupts us?' He asked.

'That is a brilliant question! You will be a great

lawyer if you hate corruption and love justice,' the Sage encouraged. 'In computing,' he continued, 'when data loses its original integrity, it is said to be corrupt. This brings about a malfunction which could even lead to a complete breakdown of the system if not remedied with an antivirus. Similarly, when humans stray off the primordial order of decency by exercizing their freewill in a manner that causes disorder or indecency, corruption is born. Such moral degradation could lead to total breakdown of society if it is not dislodged.

'Corruption is like a human virus that plagues us to justify wrongdoing. To put it succinctly, corruption is the abuse of one's freewill or right. The canker permeates the entire spectrum of the social strata but many in Masem seem to think that corruption is synonymous with political crimes. Is it only politicians who abuse their freewill or rights?' the Sage asked.

'No!' the audience replied.

'We have seen politicians who are not corrupt and we have seen corrupt people who are not politicians. There are corrupt politicians just as there are corrupt people in all professions. The decisions we make and the actions we take make the difference!' the Sage explained. 'The second part of your question is what corrupts us? Is it power, wealth or fame? The root of corruption lies at the heart of inordinate human desire,' the Sage underlined.

'Please what are some of the effects of corrupt-ion on the society and how do we eradicate corruption?' the law student again asked.

'It is difficult to quantify the cost of corruption because one corrupt act can have unpredictable ramifications. I will itemise a few of the devastating effects of corruption for you to appreciate the harrowing nature of the canker and position yourselves to fight it wherever. Here are a few:

- It satisfies the pleasure of a self-centred few and endangers the destiny of many citizens.
- It breeds lawlessness as it compromises the rule of law for the rule of inordinate desire;
- It corrodes our integrity and saps our ability to act in a right, just and acceptable manner;
- It scuttles the aspirations of nations and throws the clock of accelerated progress out of gear;
- It gnaws at the national purse and drains the gains of society;
- It grinds a nation in the throes of deprivation and makes many of her citizens to wallow in the quagmire of socio-economic stagnation;
- Corruption, like conflict, fuels the excruciating flames of dire poverty and dims the liberating torch of great prosperity.

'In the quicksand of corruption and unbridled greed, a nation is brought to ruin. In the whirlwinds of dishonesty and fraud, the soul of society is engulfed in rot.

'You also wanted to know what can be done to eradicate corruption. It begins with each and everyone of us in Masem and not only our politicians. He who is infested with corruption has no strength to fight the decay in society. He cannot offer any solution to the problem because he is the cause of it. We must be mindful of the devastating effects of corruption and in good conscience detest dishonest gain or foul play. To do this requires building sterling integrity which is a sure hedge against all forms of corruption. ' the Sage informed the audience.

'Looking at high profile cases of corruption involving the educated elite, what fundamental change in policy would you consider in our educational system for an effective response to eradicating corruption in our society?' another student asked.

'Untamed minds and hearts are weapons of social unrest and global disorder. One of the answers to our society's quest for a better world lies in inculcating in students the value of integrity above scholarship. When they gain this insight through rigorous orientation, they will be imbued with a desire to strive for integrity which is one of the high points of human achievements. They will learn integrity is not found, it is built, it is not ascribed, it is acquired. Scholarship is acclaimed, wealth is honoured, and power is feared. However, in the market place of memory, recognition and influence, the man of integrity stands tall above them all. His ovations are beyond generations,' the Sage paused and signalled to his aide to bring another bottle of water to his table.

'Great Sage, some have said that Masem is what it is because of her leaders. They explain that our leaders have failed to provide the needed leadership responsive to the challenges of the times. These days, it is common to hear people blaming leadership for almost every negative thing in Masem. I have observed growing levels of cynicism towards leadership but is it not overly simplistic to always blame leadership for our national failings?' an elderly person asked.

'I have seen people littering indiscriminately in their communities and turning around to blame leadership for poor sanitary conditions in the city. I have monitored the media and have been intrigued to hear those who blame leadership for increasing tension and violence yet their very words and conduct continue to fan flames of pandemonium. There are those who loudly decry corruption in political circles but are mute over corporate corruption and are involved in institutional fraud. What about corruption in the murky world of religion?

'Anyone can pontificate but not all can act right when presented with the opportunity to lead. Those who constantly bash leadership must find productive means to offer constructive criticism and not unproductive opprobrium. When we patronize, rundown, and condescendingly reprimand those in leadership, it does not advance the cause of nation building. Leadership is a permanent pillar of all social architecture that must be strengthened and not undermined. It is made better through constructive dialogue and criticism and must not be destroyed through unhealthy denigration and poisonous cynicism,' the Sage counselled.

'People insult and harshly criticize institutions tasked with the responsibility to enforce laws. Some state institutions have difficulty ensuring regulatory compliance because of the attitude of some citizens. What is the role of the citizen in nation building and how do we demonstrate unalloyed commitment to the rule of law?' a young lady wanted to know.

'You have brought up one of the key challenges confronting Masem in her forward march. When companies flout laws and are sanctioned by regulatory institutions, people stand up to protest against what they call "high-handedness." When members of the Politicus are arrested and made to answer charges for alleged crimes, their sympathisers mass up to demand their immediate freedom and call the arrest "witch-hunting." When violent activists are made to face the law, their followers rise up and accuse the establishment of "political intimidation." When journalists foment trouble and they are arrested by the police, their arrest is described as "attack on media freedom." There is more support for freedom but little for justice. What is the meaning of the rule of law when the law will not be allowed to rule for sanity to prevail?

'Laws are the bedrock on which a nation is built but lawlessness stifles nation building. Good citizens foster development of their nations by keeping faith with the laws of the land. Those who consistently flout laws weaken the building blocks of development and erode the foundation of advancement. We have the moral authority to expect right things to be done when we ourselves do the right things and do not blindly defend what is wrong and unlawful,' the Sage admonished them.

'Please, what will be your advice to the youth or students who have aspirations for leadership positions?' A lady questioned.

'Those with aspirations for leadership must know that the ego is a servant of gratification that trips men on the path of indiscretion. Without a listening ear and a humble heart, a leader will remain a sycophant puppet of his ego. Who will speak that he will listen? Even King Solomon with all his legendary wisdom, recognized the need for counsellors.

'By consciously deflating any over bloated sense

of self-importance, a leader will rise above leadership hubris and offer leadership that exudes C-H-A-R-A-C-T-E-R. Here, C-H-A-R-A-C-T-E-R means Courage, Humility, Accountability, Resilience, Attentiveness, Commitment, Trustworthiness, Empathy, and Responsibility. This is the kind of leadership that inspires confidence and reinvigorates the hopes and aspirations of followers. C-H-A-R-A-C-T-E-R is the proverbial ladder, by which leaders ascend and descend the rungs of greatness,' the Sage replied.

'A great man demanded my guidance on which of his children should be in charge of his vast estate. I requested a meeting with them before giving any advice on the matter. On our first meeting, I disclosed their father's intention and told them about my assignment. I gave each one of them an egg and asked them to wrap it with the piece of cloth I provided. When that was done, I told them to go home and return in a week's time. Whoever would come back with a broken egg was not worthy of the task. That was the first assignment and the next one was to follow.

'They appeared a week later as agreed and I asked who was successful with the assignment. Two confidently stepped forward but the other stayed back. I examined their eggs and asked them to tell me what made them 'successful.' They smiled and claimed they were very meticulous with the task. The one who 'failed' the assignment admitted that he must have cracked his egg the very day he took it home. This is because upon reaching home that day, he saw a crack on the egg. At this point, who deserved to inherit the estate?' the Sage asked.

'Two passed the test and so the opportunity must be given to them to go through the next stage of the exercise. The one with the broken egg has proven incapable and cannot be entrusted with the responsibility,' the audience agreed with this suggestion which came up but the Sage was to surprise them with his position.

'Many times, because we do not know the full story, we make wrong judgements. We are quick to crown 'heroes' and declare 'villains' because of the missing dimension. If only we will be willing to know the full story and appreciate the peculiar circumstances of individuals, many a time, we will be magnanimous with our judgements. The one with the broken egg deserved to be in charge of the estate and I recommended him to his father,' the Sage said.

'This is curious. Why should he be the one and not the others who have proven capable?' A lady asked.

'You can't mend a broken egg,' the Sage answered and paused for a moment. He continued, 'I gave all of them slightly cracked eggs but two came back with unbroken eggs. How could that have happened? In their desperate bid to gain prominence in the eyes of society, they suppressed honesty and trampled on their integrity. They changed the eggs thinking, it will not be noticed. Only the man with the broken egg was honest enough in spite of what he stood to lose,' the Sage revealed to the thrilled audience.

'O then, the one with the broken egg really deserved it,' they agreed.

'The youth who have aspirations for leadership positions must know that dishonesty is the bane of society. Whatever is built on lies will come crumbling. You cannot be true to others without being true to your conscience. When we remember the man with the broken egg, we will value honesty and not travesty. Becoming a leader is not great. Becoming a great leader is what counts. There are many leaders, ordinary leaders, but few great ones,' the Sage said.

CHAPTER TWELVE

Radicus became a violent maverick who caused commotion at the least provocation. He courted an unenviable reputation of a rabble-rouser who risked plunging Masem into chaos. His demeanour and public utterances continued to lend credence to the numerous assertions made by his critics who had to brace themselves for his scathing attacks.

His radical views and combative posturing reached heights of nuisance and he was ruled out as a potential winner in the race for the operations director of the IP. Contrary to such expectation, he emerged top of the contenders although his victory was saddled with suspicions of electoral fraud. Some attributed his success to the naivety of the delegates who gave him the nod without giving much thought to the individual they were selecting to be at the helm of affairs. This was one of the hazards of Masem's democracy; those without requisite conduct and competence sometimes got elected into public office.

Having lost the debate at the last leadership meeting, Radicus and his gang monitored Susubribi closely in order to set him up for a scandal. They were in a series of secret meetings throughout the week plotting Susubribi's downfall. Radicus drove to the outskirts of the city and parked at the junction where he usually met his team. He checked the time and became more restless when they delayed in showing up. His phone rang but he put it down after identifying the caller. It rang again and this was the call he had long been waiting for.

'Ok Tiger, I will get there soon,' he told him whilst lighting his cigarette. He turned on the engine and drove away from the city to meet them. After ten minutes' drive, he pulled up by the side of the road where Tiger had directed. Four muscular men clad in black emerged from the thicket and hopped in the vehicle.

'Guys, as you are aware, trouble is looming. The State Security will soon be on your trail,' Radicus informed them while driving farther away from the city.

'So what are the leaders of the party doing to protect us?' Tiger asked.

'Well, don't worry, I will . . . ' Radicus was hesitant. He was being evasive but he could not break his mould. He was harshly frank and would often say it as he saw and felt. 'Listen carefully guys,' he said bringing out a recorder from his pocket, 'let's find a place to park so we can plan our next line of action,' he told them. He veered off the road and drove through a meandering and rugged path stretching into a forest. They came to an abrupt end as a result of the thick bushes rising joining in the middle. He stopped the engine and puffed on his cigarette. Tiger stretched out his hand and picked up the cigarette box from the dashboard. He pulled out four sticks and gave one to each of his guys. He held one tightly between his lips and torched it with the lighter.

'Now, listen carefully,' Radicus said and played the recorder. 'You have now heard everything Susubribi said during the meeting. He spited and slighted me by debunking my position. He was vocal and unambiguous and he demands the immediate arrest of anyone connected with the violence irrespective of their political leanings. But I, Radicus will be very radical with him. He won the debate but he has not won the deal. He can't go the long-haul with me. I am a master strategist and will have the strategic advantage.' Radicus charged as he exhaled a cloud of cigarette smoke and quickly breathed in with widely open eyes and nose as if he was recalling the smoke back into his nostrils. 'Guys, this is the crux of the matter, Susubribi must go! As long as he remains the communications manager of our party, not even a member of this group will be spared; he is determined to crack it,' Radicus said.

Susubribi's success in life was hugely contingent upon his unflinching commitment to meeting challenges that came his way and he brought the same attitude to the political arena. He insisted brute force had no place in nation building and deployed the voice of reason to fight the canker. He galvanized support by presenting cogent arguments devoid of hatred or personal attacks. He was resolute and vowed not to cower or be cowed into inaction but Radicus and his men mounted staunch opposition to his views and questioned, 'When did he also arrive here? We were the pacesetters and we must blaze the trail!' they vowed.

'He is a political novice, who thinks he can change the political terrain. No! He will not be the one to change the face of Masem politics. We need a firebrand and fearless son of a man in charge of party communications and not that timid soul who cannot stand shoulder to shoulder with the sons of gallant men. So, you get the drift? We have to engineer his removal from the position so that he can be replaced with a ruthless individual fit for purpose,' Radicus incited the men.

'Yes! Yes!!' they exclaimed.

'We have to do what we have to do! You know the game!' Radicus said.

'We don't have much time on our hands and so the grand scheme must be hatched now!' Tiger insisted.

'We must use the media as a launch pad,' one of them suggested.

'Yes, the same modus operandi. The media is our

ally and they will always fall for anything we come up with,' Radicus agreed.

Last year, they were able to orchestrate an alleged corruption scandal against Susubribi. A number of media houses pounced on the story without digging the records to counter the false claim. Susubribi was left helplessly responding to calls from one media house to the other and he had a hard time defending his reputation.

Three months ago, they succeeded in getting a minister to resign based on an allegation of influence peddling and conflict of interest. One media house carried the cooked up story and the rest jumped on the bandwagon without doing proper independent checks to uncover the falsity of the claim. Members of the media were so fixated with breaking the news to their audience and hurried to the public without verification. They ran with the story for several weeks and unjustly portrayed the minister as a corrupt official of state. Unable to stand the unfair media trial and public ridicule, he resigned before it eventually emerged he was not complicit in any malfeasance. The media ruined his name before they realized his innocence but the damage to his reputation was hardly repaired. The excitement with which they carried the false news suddenly evaporated when they were called upon to correct the misinformation.

'We shall always succeed with fake news as long as shoddy journalism exists in the Masem media. We shall set the agenda, the media will follow and the people will believe. In this game, the media is always our ally and Susubribi can't survive it,' Radicus declared.

'Yes! The media is our strong ally and until they outgrow their inept and mediocre approach to journalism, they will continue to do our bidding,' Tiger added.

A great number of people were becoming vulnerable to media gimmicks and believed anything they heard on the airwaves. This docility coupled with a poorly regulated media space in Masem made the ground fertile for fake news to thrive. Political mischief players like Radicus and Propgantus could easily design 'scandals' against their opponents and dominate the headlines for weeks until a new story broke. Media outlets in Masem were in dire need of journalists with the kind of savvy needed to see through the agenda setting techniques of these political mischief players.

'Luscano is now on the run so we will not get him to carry this story for us as he has always done. I am meeting Propgantus this evening to decide the media platform and the journalist to push this story,' Radicus assured.

'Do you have someone we can trust to do a good job for us like Luscano?' Tiger asked.

'Don't worry. Let's leave that in the hands of Propgantus. He knows how to handle these things perfectly. Money rules the minds of these guys. When we pay them, you will be shocked to see how they will sustain the agenda without backing out easily. Even when it becomes obvious they have misinformed the public, they will not easily accept criticism and humbly apologize. In order to protect their egos they will resort to obfuscating matters instead of simply retracting the story. When this happens, we would have achieved our aim,' Radicus ended.

CHAPTER THIRTEEN

A section of the Religis in Masem held the view that religious matters were beyond the scope of ordinary minds and so instructions from certain leaders of the Religis were expected to be followed without questioning. This perception gave rise to unenlightened consensus that was inadvertently promoting religious scams within the Masem society.

In certain quarters, activities of some members of the Religis were becoming more of a curse rather than a blessing to adherents who got swindled in their pursuit of faith. With greed fuelling their creed, some of these charlatans parading as 'spiritual emissaries' continued to defraud and exploit unsuspecting followers who had been rendered vulnerable and gullible on the altar of blinding faith.

Calls for proper regulation of religious affairs in Masem were ignored on the grounds that matters of religion transcended the realm of secular authority and that a high degree of laxity was required in dealing with activities of the Religis.

Holisurf was an infamous member of the Religis who often agitated the minds of the people with questionable claims. He had established himself as a 'man of God' and announced His mantra, 'holy servant' wherever he went. He insisted his name was Holiserv, meaning holy servant and not

Holisurf which had taken over his real name. But the people continued to call him Holisurf arguing, his claimed holiness was only on the surface and that he was full of religion but less of spirituality.

Whenever he was provoked, he would raise his two hands up over his head as if he was going to roll on the floor and threaten, 'nobody messes with Holiserv, the holy servant of God.' He had claimed that if his hands were raised for more than a minute, whoever was troubling him would be struck by 'spiritual hands' unless his anger was appeased. This was widely rumoured but never witnessed although his hands were raised on countless occasions.

Aside allegations of building a fortune on the ignorance of his followers, he harped on superstition to hold their minds in perpetual allegiance. He infused them with fear by propagating mythologies that enslaved the minds of the ardent ones. They were brainwashed to believe 'spiritual enemies' were responsible for their challenges in life and so they needed Holisurf to break the front of the so called spiritual adversaries. He was accused of splitting several relationships including marriages based on his frenzy declarations of 'spiritual enemies.'

A young man who had lost his job contacted Holisurf who directed that he fast and pray for eleven days. He assured he was going to 'break an ancestral jinx' plaguing the young man's success.

In the course of fasting, the young man fainted and nearly died of starvation if he had not been rushed to the hospital for resuscitation. It was later established he was fired for acts of indolence. His supervisors often found him idling about while others were busily working. All he needed to do was to eschew laziness for God to bless the work of his hands.

A lady also approached Holisurf and told him she had been in constant squabbles with her husband and needed his intervention. He gave her a bill of items she needed to buy to enable him wage 'spiritual war' against the 'spiritual enemies' in her family who he claimed, were plotting her divorce. Meanwhile, close relations of the lady knew her pride was her plight. She had an attitudinal challenge that required a deliberate effort at working on her pride in order to save her marriage but Holisurf blamed it on imaginary enemies

Those who were influenced by his religious persuasions lived with hallucinated fear of mythical enemies only to be ruined by their own hubris. They were yet to learn that whether they were going to rise in sainthood or fall for impiety, they were their own actors, standing on the stage of their freewill. This reality was completely lost on them and so they continued to blame their own failings on machinations of 'spiritual enemies.' In denial of realities which required practical action escapist tales propagated by Holisurf and certain leaders of the Religis.

His followers battling with financial challenges approached him and said, 'Servant of God, you always announce that people should come for financial breakthrough but we have been here for ages and cannot break through. Please what should we do?'

'Have I not been telling you that blessed are the poor in spirit? Your treasures are not on earth! O why are you so soon descending into the realms of carnal cravings? Ignore the material and focus on your spiritual needs! Be spiritual! Just believe and have faith, you are blessed!! Receive it!!!' Holisurf preached. Those who were convinced by what he said responded 'amen' and went away singing but others were unmoved and wanted to ask more questions.

Holisurf had built financial empire in Masem and was far away from the shores of scarcity. If being poor alone could warrant blessings as he claimed, why was he focused on accumulating wealth and not willing to share the fate of the poor? Even though their poverty had reached threatening levels, his trumpeting of 'blessed are the poor' became a tranquilising phrase that lulled them into economic inertia. But they came to the realization that poverty was a challenge that needed to be confronted but not to be extolled.

'I don't need money for anything except the

work of God,' Holisurf told those who were not convinced by his earlier explanation.

'But we also contribute from the little we get from our work. If we break through we can contribute huge sums,' one of them insisted.

'Don't worry, I will pray for you but keep bringing the little you have and don't forget to increase it when more money comes. This night, the prayer session is going to be against spiritual enemies fighting prosperity. Don't miss it, your breakthrough is here,' he urged.

CHAPTER FOURTEEN

It was 11pm but Holisurf and his followers were at it again with their usual all night service. The jarring noise that hung in the air disturbed creativity. The vicinity was enveloped in piercing sounds of spontaneous screams, claps and drums that posed grave health hazards to citizens. Day and night, they disturbed the inhabitants of Masem with excessive noise emanating from their religious activities and those who complained were tagged as 'spiritual enemies.'

Noise pollution in some parts of the city reached a breaking point but the authorities tasked to check this were yet to scale the challenge of institutional incompetence. Holisurf assumed a no-nonsense personality in the neighbourhood, riding roughshod over his own elders and the community council. He continued to defy restrictions placed on excessive noise making but numerous complaints from the community pushed some of his elders to have further engagement with him on the matter.

'Servant of God, we admit that the complaints from the community are legitimate. Serenity contributes to good health and helps the sick to recover speedily and so let's stop disturbing the sick in the community hospital. The teachers in the nearby school have often come here to express displeasure about the noise we generate. A disturbed mind cannot absorb knowledge so we have to reduce the noise for the children to learn. Others have also come to complain that they return from work with the hope of coming home to rest only to be met with blaring noise from our programmes. This, according to them, has disturbed their sleep and resulted in health complications. Our refusal to heed the numerous complaints would mean we are not sensitive to the plight of our neighbours. If we love our neighbours, we must not disturb them.' Holisurf was advised by one of his elders.

'I am not here to please men but God! I don't care what the people say!' As usual, Holisurf ignored the criticisms and questioned, 'Who are you to mess with Holiserv?'

'Please are you saying we can't minimise the noise? In our study of Elijah's contest with the prophets of Baal, we learnt it did not require loud shouts to invoke fire from God to burn the sacrifice. When Elijah approached the altar and calmly prayed, God answered by sending fire to burn his sacrifice. One lesson is clear but we have failed to grasp; we do not have to shout for God to hear us. God is not commanded by loud shouts,' one of the elders added but that angered Holisurf the more.

'Ah! I can smell the conspiracy of my spiritual enemies. Now that all of you are singing the song of traitors, I would rather wish we part company than be betrayed. Nobody messes with Holiserv. You are no more part of us! This is the door!' Holisurf displayed zealous religious antics but lacked humility in dealing with even his own elders.

He was summoned to a meeting of the Community Council for persistently ignoring their complaints. Accompanied by three of his followers, he stormed the gathering already provoked for a showdown. 'If they continue to exhibit unbelief, they will see my dark side. If they provoke me and I raise my hands, they will see what they have not seen before,' he hinted before entering the meeting.

'Holisurf,' one of the Council members addressed him, 'we summoned you...'

'I am Holiserv, not Holisurf!' he interrupted.

'But you are known all over as Holisurf,' one elder insisted.

'That is why I say I live in the midst of corrupt people. Look at how you have even corrupted my name. The evidence of your corruption is so glaring and I can bear testimony before God!' His reply generated a great uproar of laughter and murmurs from the gathering.

'OK, that is not why we called you here. You have consistently defied our earlier instructions by continuing with your incessant noisemaking activities in this community. This meeting serves as the last in a series of efforts made in order to have your cooperation. Reason with us this time or we go to court for a restraining order to compel you...'

'Who can order Holiserv, the holy servant of God?' he retorted. 'I am not under the law!' he told them.

'God is the source of law and order! The lawless cannot serve God! As long as you live in this community, you have no choice in this matter than to be law abiding. It is only by so doing that we can build the nation,' one elder rebuked him and shot down his argument.

'Hahaha...You and who will build the nation?' Holisurf retorted. 'Let me enlighten you here if you don't know spiritual matters. Have you not read or been told that except the Lord builds, the builders build in vain? No man can build the nation only God can! We can only pray and wait for his intervention! That is why you have to honour some of us who have dedicated ourselves to fasting and prayers, all nights and all days to secure the interest of the nation. You are mere mortals who strive with men but we are in the arena of higher realms, waging spiritual battles; breaking and binding that which flesh and blood cannot contend with,' as always, Holisurf showcased boastful sophistry.

'O Holisurf, I am completely appalled by your literal understanding of the text you paraphrased. With a limited understanding of scripture, it will be better for you to be a student than a teacher. Don't deceive yourself and mislead your followers,' one elder cautioned. 'Where did you learn that human effort is meaningless as far as nation building is concerned? When your house is set on fire will you just stand and pray or you will make an effort to put out the flames? Will divine intervention come to the man who makes no effort? We have a role to play in nation building and we cannot shirk that responsibility by listening to confusing interpretations of scriptural texts. We have to do what is right to brighten our world with sanity and orderliness. That is the meaning of nation building,' the elder reiterated.

'Be careful how you speak confidently about spiritual matters from the position of a layman. Do you know how I got my call? If you knew my spiritual level, you wouldn't even have the courage to speak with me this way. Mind you, nobody messes with Holiserv! Pray for your eyes and ears to open so that you will see and hear what I have been seeing and hearing. Let me reveal this to you, the sounds that emanate from our prayer services are not noise as you perceive. Spiritually, they are sounds of triumph in higher realms. O you unbelievers, just believe and have faith!' Holisurf preached.

'Just believe and have faith'... has that not been your tool for deception? 'Just believe and have faith'... are we that gullible to believe whatever we are told or too weak to accept any instruction? No! Holisurf, we can't just believe and have faith as you have always insisted,' the chairperson of the Community Council told him. He added, 'God gave us a mind to think and a conscience to reason and so faith must not blind our minds where reason is required. The noise in this community is becoming too much and no amount of 'faith' can change this reality. Stop the noise for us to have peace in this community. If you are unwilling to comply with persuasion, we would apply force in the coming days,' he warned Holisurf.

Holisurf raised his two hands as usual and walked out of the meeting shouting, 'nobody messes with Holiserv...!'

CHAPTER FIFTEEN

Mongris was indiscreet and demonstrated a seeming irresistible urge for loose talk. He remained overly active on social media and merrily relayed trending news whenever they gathered and chatted at the Town Square where current issues never missed the wagging and bragging tongue of the youth. 'I am a citizen journalist,' he often touted as he unknowingly circulated lies and social media pranks. Whenever he shared false information or rehashed a rumour and was asked to provide strict proof, he would say, 'O it is all over on social media.'

Social media continued to gain grounds in Masem as the technology brought enormous innovation for marketing and business communication. But the technological gift was also on a path of a social revolution that posed a serious threat to social harmony, governance and leadership. Social media was becoming a technological conundrum promoting social maladies in various quarters. It granted licence for mass gossip and trading in fake news; destroying the reputations of great citizens, leaders, organizations and businesses. Increasingly, the cyberspace was being hijacked for hate speeches, vilification, vulgarity, fraud and numerous nation-wrecking activities.

A year ago, Masem witnessed a full-blown crisis

triggered by social media content. But for the rapid response from the security agencies, that could have marked the beginning of Masem's cyber war.

For political advantage, sham politicians produced materials aimed at damaging their opponents and circulated them through cyberspace. These viciously contrived contents did irreparable damage to people's hard-earned reputation, leaving their victims in the throes of emotional havoc.

Behind cyber timidity emboldened by anonymity, some individuals and groups of persons engaged in hate mongering and subversive advocacies, posing grave security risks to Masem and jeopardizing her stability. Calls for stricter control and regulation to deal with promoters of cyber deviance grew and authorities considered deploying cyber intelligence to counter the technological menace.

By 3pm, social media was trending with news of Susubribi's arrest. The airwaves were also inundated with commentaries full of mindless mockery from his political opponents who had become experts at predicting doom and gloom. They pontificated on the story as though they were repositories of insight. In a short space of time, his reputation had been shredded and hanged on the gallows of frenzied emotions.

His family and loved ones were disturbed by the

barrage of media pronouncements that tilted towards condemnations. Even before a court of competent jurisdiction would sit on the matter, certain courts in the arena of public opinion had already ruled and declared him guilty. Some civil society organizations (CSOs) could not stand above the fray and also started issuing statements by taking contentious positions on a matter that was yet to be properly investigated. In the name of public interest advocacy, they hastily condemned him based on mere suspicion of wrongdoing.

In a few hours, Susubribi who stood for decent politics had become a victim of brutish political machinations. Before the party hierarchy would issue a news release, media outlets had broken the news of Susubribi's resignation as the Communications Manager of the IP.

He was heartlessly sneered at and jeered in the media by those who regrettably behaved as if accusations were akin to complicity. They pre-empted the outcome of the investigations and repeated their prejudiced narratives to influence the often hasty verdict of public opinion, ignoring that the court of public opinion could never be a good substitute for the court of competent jurisdiction.

Mongris got wind of the developing story and took to social media by circulating pictures of Susubribi with ridiculous captions. He rushed to the Town Square that evening to continue stoking the ember of hearsay.

'Have you heard Susubribi is in the grips of the police for some criminal conduct?' Mongris asked before looking for a place to sit.

'Yes, I have been monitoring media reports for more details to know his exact offence. As it stands now, there is little information for one to jump to conclusions,' the moderator replied.

'He will surely be jailed because he was in possession of a fake passport and that warranted his arrest at the airport. I can't understand why such a high ranking public figure would travel with fraudulent documents. Ah! These corrupt politicians, are they under any spell to be corrupt or what?' Mongris condemned, hoping to elicit interest.

'Mongris, the man has been arrested for an alleged crime and we don't have all the details. Let us be careful how we run commentaries on matters we have limited knowledge of. In the absence of facts and certainty, don't fill the vacuum with speculations and conjectures! Let us suspend all hasty judgements for proper determination of the case to enable us speak to the issues from an informed position. You can't arrive at an unblemished position without dispassionately evaluating information,' the moderator advised him.

'O you are saying this because you have not keenly followed traditional and social media reports. Fresh details emerging indicate he will be grilled for other shady deals. People will come to know why his businesses are thriving. You don't know how corrupt politicians cover up their tracks. Even if he is eventually left off the hook, I Mongris will not believe that he is clean. I cannot be deceived!' Mongris maintained.

Cynicism was becoming the new religion of people like Mongris who got glued to their preconceived notions in spite of the glaring evidence that eventually popped up to challenge their pitched positions. In their view, rumours were 'the truth' or 'the facts' and any contrary information that emerged to challenge the rumour was considered false. They were more prone to believing and spreading lies and inaccuracies than accepting and propagating what was true and accurate. When some accused persons were convicted after investigations, they praised the police for doing a great job but whenever certain suspects were cleared after investigations, they alleged a cover-up and accused the police of unprofessional conduct.

Susubribi had recorded global footprints with his career before joining Masem politics and his exploits had brought honour and recognition to Masem. Those who knew him very well could vouch for his integrity without a second thought. They were yet to come to terms with his arrest but in the camp of cynics, presumption of guilt was preferred to that of innocence.

'I have been listening to Lawyer Propgantus on several networks and he is sure that Susubribi will be implicated. You cannot downplay the legal opinion of Lawyer Propgantus who knows the law,' Mongris stated.

'O Mongris! Don't just listen, but listen critically. Aren't we in Masem? Don't we know Propgantus? This is someone whose legal arguments persistently advance his political cause above the national good. Yes, he is a lawyer but don't be swindled by the titles that adorn the names of men, check their conduct. Great lawyers are consistently guided by principles of law and the rational consideration of nation building. Any time they speak or write, there is no tinge of bias or unprofessionalism in their appreciation of issues. If you care to know and be on guard, you will learn that there are lawless lawyers and unjust judges who trade the national interest for parochial advantage. We have been keenly following developments in Masem and we know those, whose political parties mean more to them than the nation that gave birth to them,' the moderator said.

'Anyway, I am reliably informed that Susubribi will spend not less than five years in prison if he is convicted. Ah, just imagine the collateral disgrace he will suffer. Why bring such humiliation upon yourself and family? I would have cut all ties with him if he were my friend,' Mongris said scornfully.

'Mongris, what is there to gain in being mean-spirited? Wish your neighbour's progress and never his fall. Should he even stumble and fall, his fall should never be the object of your glee. We sink into the debasing malaise of crass insensitivity when we gloat over the misfortune of others. Fellow-feeling gets buried in the pit of callousness when we gleefully castigate or ridicule persons charged with offences or those convicted of certain crimes. Sympathy and compassion are eternal values that build a nation. Vicious ill-will and malicious gratification are destructive missiles that can bring a nation to rubble,' the moderator advised Mongris.

CHAPTER SIXTEEN

The Masem society had long outpaced the days when propaganda held sway on the minds of the masses. But Propgantus remained a sleazy and sneaky politician steeped in the politics of fabrication and rancour. His unrefined language and persistent peddling of lies triggered ceaseless public relations quagmires which continued to dent the image of the IP. His entry into the IP's communication team was met with stiff resistance from key functionaries of the party who insisted it will be politically suicidal to make him a party communicator. Nonetheless, some leaders, including Radicus lobbied for him to join the team to help them project their agenda.

A few years on, the verdict was obvious; he had lost relevance in national conversations with a track record that spoke volumes about the length he had travelled on the path of treachery and impropriety. The hot chase for power and recognition at the expense of his integrity saw him sinking speedily into the depths of self-mockery and disdain. He approached issues with overly skewed political lenses and so, the more he spoke, the more he lost the ears of critical thinkers. His ranting and ravings on media platforms were aimed at swaying public opinion to secure electoral fortunes but his inward-looking analysis and hollow arguments had no air of gravitas to influence well-meaning citizens. Propgantus became notorious for smear campaigns, hate speeches and strategic incitements but he confused notoriety with popularity and so, in spite of the shame, he mistook it for fame.

He met his team and told them of his determination to become the communications manager of the IP. The backroom manoeuvrings by Radicus inspired his hope of a tremendous victory in spite of leadership kicking against his intention.

'I am the most youthful among the various contenders in this race and so let this message be communicated clearly for the delegates to know that the future belongs to the youth and not old men who need to sit back and rest.' Propgantus arrogantly made these declarations as his team busily wrote down what he reeled-off as strategies for his campaign.

'The future belongs to the youth,' he often boasted but lacked the wisdom and humility to accept that the young needed to learn from the old in order to receive the baton of honed leadership. Blinded by politics without cultured-decency, he denigrated old age as though he was destined to remain young forever.

When politics opened doors for him to rub shoulders with the elderly, he turned around to disrespect even those who could give birth to him. He departed from the values that brought honour and recognition to one's place of birth. By lowering the standards of public discourse, he mired committed patriots in the arena of verbal assaults.

The peace and development of the nation came second to his party's electoral fortunes and this was demonstrated through his persistent attacks on certain individuals and institutions. In his desperation, he blew both sensitive and trivial issues out of proportion and muddied the image of his nation globally. He would lie and defend the indefensible even when some of his colleagues were communicating a contrary position. This exposed him as an unprincipled person who would say anything in pursuit of power and recognition. He became a known political chameleon who changed his position on issues at will depending on who was involved or which political party it affected.

Laymen would have thought that lawyers, by their training, would have been ardent ambassadors of law and order in all societies. But Propgantus made those who thought this way rethink their assumption and reconsider such an erroneous conclusion. His conduct was uncharacteristic of a member of the 'learned' fraternity and his behaviour brought home the realization that the study of law alone did not make one lawful but self-discipline was what produced well-behaved citizens.

He appeared completely oblivious of the important place the courts occupied in all orderly societies and seemed not to appreciate the fact that without the courts to adjudicate on disputes, there would have been no bastion of the rule of law. Blinded by political zealousness, he did not see the danger in running down the institution that protected society against disorder and injustice. Whenever his party or any of their members lost a case in court, he took to the media and cast a slur on the integrity of the judges that sat upon the case.

However, any time his party or any of their members won a case, he turned around to urge all to 'Respect the decision of the courts and honour the competent judges for their wisdom and ruling on the matter.' His political opponents standing trial for corruption charges were 'Corrupt officials fit for jail,' but members of his party charged with similar offences were 'Heroes being persecuted by the establishment' and their trials were nothing but 'Malicious political retributions.'

Propgantus hopped from one media house to the other discrediting due judicial process and covertly engineering lawless defiance. All of these resulted in complete erosion of his credibility to the extent that discerning members of his party did not find him attractive to hold any key position going into the future.

At a leadership meeting of the IP, one influential

elder told the gathering, 'In selecting people to serve in critical roles, the IP must not depart from our renowned position as an organization with decent ethos. What should be our topmost consideration when choosing people to serve in leadership capacities? Do we go for someone who will help us build the nation or the one who will help us win elections? Do we gamble with our integrity by choosing someone who falls below the standard of decorum and decency required in public discourse? Politics is a nation-building venture and not an election-winning adventure; this thinking must always inform our choice of leaders. We need those who communicate with candour and respect and not the type that unleash verbal attacks.

'Our claim of building the nation will be brought into question if we leave party leadership in the hands of dishonest and unprincipled individuals. Their style of communication belongs to the primitive era of politics, and we can't build a nation with brutal, dishonest and reckless communicators. Their penchant for denigrating and insulting opponents is unhealthy for nation building and people like that in our party must be taught that constructive criticism required for nation building cannot be exchanged for destructive criticism and debilitating intolerance.

'We have railroaded some persons into the communications team but we cannot repeat that mistake by making any of such individuals become head of party communications. People can be intelligent but if they lack integrity, they must not be the mouthpiece of any great organization. Let's not make the mistake of our opponents who have prioritized elections and are struggling with high levels of indiscipline because of the calibre of leadership within their ranks,' the elder stated.

Against a backdrop of stiff opposition to his ambition, Propgantus was determined to run for the position. He refused to step aside and went ahead with his campaign. 'They know that I will win so they have started prevailing on me not to contest. Do you agree that I back out?' he asked his team.

'No! No! No!' they protested.

'As you all can see, I am well versed in matters of law and can stand our opponents in any policy or governance debate,' Propgantus boasted.

'That's why we say, Lawyer Propgantus is the man to vote for! Lawyer Propgantus is a member of the intelligentsia! Don't mind them, you are the incoming Communications Manager of the IP,' a member of his campaign team hailed. By remaining impervious to advice, he often enjoyed praise singing which in the end brought embarrassment but he was lost to shame.

Propgantus aimed at climbing the higher rungs of leadership but failed to learn that excessive doses of praise could cloud the clarity of even a clear-eyed leader. He did not know that praise singing often celebrated mediocrity but constructive criticism fostered excellence. He would often deflect criticisms by saying, 'I don't listen to critics; their voices are discordant notes in the melody of pleasure. His ego was his traitor preventing him from accepting meaningful criticisms that could have prepared him for greatness. He shunned the discomfort of honesty and found himself in the illusory solace of flattery.

'Propgantus is a member of the intelligentsia! Whether they like you or hate you, you will be the winner come the election day!' Someone shouted from his team.

'Thank you for recognizing a genius. You are a wise man. The ignorant cannot appreciate the stuff that I am made of and so they always want to criticize me. I am putting myself up for the position in order to serve your interests. If not for the good of the party and yourselves, I would not have worried myself at all. The party belongs to all of you and so you must also enjoy some of her benefits. You need me there to fight for you! Next week by this time, I will be declared Communications Manager of our party,' he told his highly excited team.

CHAPTER SEVENTEEN

'Guys, I salute you for such a smart move. I am convinced that no amount of police investigations will be able to unravel the facts of the matter. A great job is done! Susubribi is gone!' Radicus expressed delight at the outcome of their scheme. Susubribi had long been critical of their radical engagements and hounding him out of the party had long been conceived.

'How to get our own man in charge of the communications team is our next challenge but you all agree with me that Propgantus is the right man for the position. Don't you?' he asked.

'Yes! Yes!' they replied.

'He is the one who can galvanize our militant grassroots and whip up their zeal to go all out in defence of the party. We will use violence where it demands and diplomacy where it is required. However, be careful, never shed human blood. As far as I know, there is no peace for the soul that takes the life of another. The crime of murder is a burden too heavy for any human to carry,' Radicus warned.

'Then we should stop our violent operations, if not, we may inadvertently commit murder,' Tiger declared.

'The ignorant speaks boldly about what he thinks he knows. You wouldn't say what you just said if you know what I have been exposed to.

I have masterfully engineered a number of violent operations but a few went bad. I have been in this game for a while and I know how to keep these things under control. Let them present their strongest arguments to win the people and we will unleash intimidation; our powerful bargaining tool,' Radicus stated.

'I don't know what you know but what I do know is that violence and bloodshed are neighbours. There is just a thin line for one to cross over from violence to shedding blood,' Tiger clarified.

'For that I agree with you. It reminds me of what some wise men have told me,' Radicus admitted. Hardly would he make such concessions. 'I don't know why this thing keeps coming up but today I will share this information with you. I once visited a wise man with the expectation of being told how to become one of the movers and shakers of Masem. It took me seven years of frantic efforts to finally get the rare opportunity to meet him.

After traversing many territories to reach his destination, it took seven days for me to finally meet him face to face. When I finally met him, it took seven minutes for him to speak to me and when he finally spoke, he uttered only seven words. "Never shed human blood in your life!" He warned. I sat for minutes hoping to hear something more, but he never spoke. I left the cottage highly frustrated and confused because what he told me was not what my ears were eager to hear. Why would he warn me against such a heinous crime as murder? I cannot contemplate committing murder let alone to carry it out.

'I visited the Sage of Masem to help me decode the words of the wise man. I still could not understand why the wise man would warn me against what I was not predisposed to. The Sage sat for minutes and finally told me that unrestrained anger could lead one to commit a crime he never intended. He cautioned me to shun violence so as to prevent shedding human blood. "Anger and violence have courted many to commit crimes they never intended. Tame your anger, hate violence, and you will never come close to murder." Those were his specific words.

'Why should my anger be tamed when people keep making me angry and how do I hate violence when people provoke me to act? Those who make me angry will feel my wrath and those who provoke me to act will have a taste of violence in a measure proportional to their provocation. I have to tame them. I was candid about my philosophy but the Sage looked at me in the face and said, "Radicus, your true strength is not determined by how you flex your muscles but your ability to submit yourself to decency no matter the level of provocation. Your job is to tame your negative inclinations and not to tame others. Go and work on your temperament and be careful you do not ignore the warning couched in those seven words. The hot-headed discovers sobriety only in moments of calamity but don't become a victim of what you can prevent. You have been exposed to your flaw which could herald your fall," the Sage also warned.

'I regret telling my wife about my encounter with the wise man and the Sage of Masem because she has inscribed the words of the sage on a board and placed it at the entrance to my hall to daily remind me that; ANGER AND VIOLENCE HAVE COURTED MANY TO COMMIT CRIMES THEY NEVER INTENDED. TAME YOUR ANGER, HATE VIOLENCE AND YOU WILL NEVER COME CLOSE TO MURDER. I see this inscription everyday but it does not bode well with me. Guys, we will not kill but we will show them that we are men. Those who stand in our way must be intimidated even if it means subjecting them to bodily harm. We have to tame them!

'Now listen, leadership is bent on sidelining Propgantus. We were in a meeting and all indications point to the fact that Propgantus is not their favourite. We have to tame them to get what we want and we will resist any attempt to fill the vacancy except our desire is honoured. At all cost, this operation must not fail!' Radicus incited.

***

Full-scale investigations launched into Susubribi's case led to the arrest of four suspects connected with the set up. They confessed swapping his original passport for a fake one. Susubribi was vindicated by the evidence gathered by the police and cleared of any wrong doing. Leadership of the party met to consider his recall and the idea received a groundswell of support from leading members of the IP except the caucus led by Radicus. They were unimpressed and hotly registered their opposition to get leadership to rescind the decision that had been firmed up.

Radicus instructed Tiger to garner some numbers to stage a protest in the streets. He was also directed to terrorize Susubribi so much so that he would willingly decline the position. 'Tame him and anyone who stands in our way! I assure you, if this operation succeeds, you will receive a handsome financial reward. Do not fail!'

Agitations began snowballing when news of Susubribi's intended reinstatement hit media headlines. Puppet demonstrators surged into the streets to protest Susubribi's comeback. This was done in allegiance to the demands of their political godfathers who were pulling the strings. They destroyed anything in their way as they marched to a radio station where Susubribi was granting interview.

The milling crowd of militant activists chanted songs as some rushed into the building to drive him out of the studios. The security men at the station flanked him and whisked him out of the building through an emergency exit. Amidst heckling, he was escorted to his car but the mob tried to prevent him from moving out of the yard. The thugs followed and smashed his windscreen before he could speed off.

Four of the men jumped onto motorbikes and pursued him even as he tried to drive away from the chaotic scene. They were bent on closing in on him and gave him a hot chase. Onlookers were shocked by the naked show of lawlessness being displayed by the thugs in broad daylight. 'Boom! Boom! Boom!' Multiple gunshots were fired in full view of glaring eyes.

'Is this Masem or a lawless territory?' An old lady was heard expressing her disgust.

'How do people get such brazen courage to showcase this level of jungle buffoonery?' A man also asked. The scandalous incident unleashed a torrent of reactions of frustration and rage from alarmed and helpless citizens.

He drove at lightning speed to seek refuge at the police station when he realized his life was in danger. Driving at such a high speed made him think he would soon be out of the close-range danger that was looming but his assailants closed the gap no matter hard he tried to widen the pace. Confusion engulfed him as he came close to negotiating the sharp curve in the centre of the city. Slowing down to negotiate the curve was as risky as negotiating without slowing down but as another gunshot was fired, he was left with the option of speeding without slowing down. A loud blast from the tyre shot through his ears and sent him struggling to regain control of the vehicle that had veered off its lane.

Within minutes, the city was crawling with apprehension as many people poured out into the streets to witness the gory accident. They surged forward to get close to the scene but the police arrived in a flash and cordoned off the area to prevent the crime trail from being tampered with. Stricken with fear and rage, the crowd vented their irritation in an outburst of accusations. Leadership inertia on the part of the political establishment, according to some of them, had accounted for growing levels of sheer lawlessness in Masem.

'You cannot rule out leadership complicity for all of these. They have not been able to deal ruthlessly with those who continue to disrupt order in the society,' one man complained.

'Why do you blame government for people's acts of lawlessness? The attack on Susubribi is a clear case of criminal activity and it must be described as such. Let us condemn acts of crime and not seek to rationalize them by blaming leadership as if individual responsibility does not exist in this society. We must support the police with valuable information to fight crime in our communities and stop playing to the gallery of political folly,' another person challenged.

CHAPTER EIGHTEEN

The youth at the Town Square were disgusted to hear no arrest had been made in connection with the attack on Susubribi. Whispers of suspicion alleged the culprits were being shielded by highly placed political actors.

'The law must prevail for the good of our society! There should be no compromise!' one Town Square member maintained.

'I agree with you. We need to advocate enforcement of every minute law that sits on any page of our law books to advance an orderly society. This is what fans my interest in politics. I want to join the bureaucrats in Masem to help build the nation,' another member indicated.

'This is a great intention and it is well thought out but be careful you don't become a public lord when you join our bureaucrats,' the secretary cautioned.

'Please come clear, who is a public lord?' another member asked. 'Public servants serve the interests of the public but public lords serve their own interests at the expense of the public. Leadership is not a call to self-service but an opportunity to respond to the needs of the people,' the secretary clarified.

'That is a great advice. If all those jostling for positions in our society were to be so minded, many would have conducted themselves in ways that lessen the burden of the downtrodden. When you critically assess the conduct and utterances of some of our bureaucrats and those vying to become part of the establishment, you wonder if they have what it takes to be leaders of our nation,' the moderator of the meeting stated.

'It seems you all don't have information on those behind the attack on Susubribi. I have the latest on that story,' Mongris informed them. 'I have gathered some intelligence on the matter and you will be shocked to know that the demonstration leading to his attack was masterminded by some key members of the IP,' he revealed.

'This is very intriguing but are there factions within the IP to trigger this senseless demonstration? Who thinks Susubribri is not suitable for the position and wants to see his back? How did you get to know this Mongris?' Someone inquired.

'Hahaha... are you surprised? I am abreast of the times. I have reliable sources who feed me with information. Don't forget that I am a citizen journalist and I can tell you more than you know,' Mongris bragged. 'Journalism was always at the top of my career aspirations but I had to jettison that ambition at a certain point in time and consider going into business. I will study for a degree and become a professional journalist,' Mongris said.

'Will you go for a Bachelor of Arts in Communications with a major in Journalism?' another asked.

'Hahaha . . . it reminds me of someone who said, "I am married and so what will I use a bachelor's certificate for? It is for bachelors!" Mongris humoured them. 'Okay, back to what I was saying, I know the one behind the attack on Susubribi but I don't want to assist the police,' he hinted.

'Citizens must wake up to their civic responsibilities and so if we have any information that will assist in fighting crimes in our communities, we should be willing to alert relevant state institutions. Suspicious characters within our societies must not be left unreported. Members of this Town Square should be very keen on ensuring order in our communities. Who must have triggered this violent demonstration? Mongris, do you know? ' the moderator inquired.

'O but this is an open secret to anyone with his ears on the ground. I will not be the one to give leads to the police to establish that Radicus is the prime suspect in this matter. I don't want trouble and so I will not stick my neck out to report him. I cannot stand the frustration that the police will subject me to for willingly volunteering information. When we meet here, I am able to tell you a lot or when I call into a radio programme, I can share a lot but I will not go to any institution to give information because they won't pay me for that service,' Mongris explained.

'What is your contribution to nation building if you can't genuinely help your nation to fight crime? Be a responsible citizen Mongris,' someone told him.

'You always talk about the citizens and forget the villagers,' Mongris gave another joke. The Town Square meeting was over and members dispersed, but a scuffle broke out and all rushed out to see.

'Today, I will teach you to mind your own business,' an angry young man warned as he clung to the collar of Mongris and pressed him against the wall.

'If you don't leave me I will wound you!' Mongris threatened but he was hurled to the ground before people could step in to separate them.

'Don't try me next time or you will see the fierce part of me!' Mongris bragged after he had been rescued.

'Why did you do that to Mongris?' the young man was questioned.

'He went about spreading rumours about me on social media and that is why I confronted him,' he replied.

'If you can live in peace with many things that don't get to your ears, why can't you be at ease with the few that get to your ears? Remember we are here to build bridges, not to break them. Value relationships but don't destroy them. It is not a noble act to fight,' he was rebuked by an elderly man.

***

The four suspects who were picked up were being quizzed at the police headquarters. 'Bring their leader,' the Police Commander began interrogating the leader of the gang.

'What is your name?' she asked.

'Tiger' he replied.

'What was your mission at the radio station?'

'I was there to drive Susubribi out of the station.'

'What authority did you have to lead a team to drive him out?'

'I was working under the instruction of my boss.'

'Who is your boss?'

'Radicus' he answered.

'What would have been his interest?' she probed further to extract more information from the leader of the gang.

'He wanted Susubribi out as the Communications Manager,' Tiger replied.

'What happened when you chased him out of the radio station?'

'We followed him with a motorbike until the accident occurred.'

'How did the accident occur?' she asked, but Tiger was hesitant.

'I have told you that we need your maximum cooperation. Do not fail to give us all the information we need from you,' she demanded.

'We shot the tyre of his vehicle and so when he tried to swerve from ramming into the storey building, his vehicle collided with a salon car that suddenly emerged from the sharp curve,' Tiger replied.

'What did you do after the accident?'

'We had to escape the scene so…'

'So…?' the Commander asked.

'We had to escape the scene,' Tiger maintained.

'What were you chasing him for?'

'We wanted to tame him to reject the position.'

'What was your motivation in all of these?'

'We were promised some money and other fringe benefits,' Tiger revealed.

'All of you are energetic guys who can channel your energies into productive ventures to help your families and communities but you have sold your freedom to a life of violence and crime. What is there to gain in criminal acts except a life of shame and regret? Okay, take him back to the cell and bring the next suspect,' she instructed.

CHAPTER NINETEEN

Radicus was surprised to find that his wife and children had not returned when he got home. He picked up his phone and dialled her number but she could not be reached. He checked the time again and it was already past 7pm. A mood of uneasiness descended on him as he kept monitoring the gate to see who would enter. He hurried to the gate when he heard the purr of a car engine. It was Propgantus.

'What time are we leaving?' he asked.

'My wife and the children have still not returned. Let's wait for them before we leave. I am certain they will arrive soon,' Radicus assured. He was quick to pick up the phone when a call finally came through. 'Please report at the Masem General Hospital immediately . . . ,' a strange voice on the line informed him.

'What is the . . . ' He wanted more details but the caller hanged up abruptly. He could still sense the urgency in her tone. He hurried to his car and sped off to the hospital accompanied by Propgantus. A nurse met them at the reception and took them to a waiting room.

'I hope all is well?' Radicus asked but the nurse would not give an answer.

'Please wait for a moment here. The doctor will meet you soon,' she indicated in a brisk voice as she flung the door close behind her. His head began to ache with nervousness as clouds of ominous uncertainty enveloped his whole being. He kept pacing back and forth until a doctor burst into the waiting room and demanded, 'Who is Radicus?'

'I am the one Doctor. Where is my family?' he asked, looking straight into the eyes of the doctor.

'Follow me,' the doctor demanded. They followed him to the Emergency Ward where he asked them to wait for a moment. In a few minutes, he returned with two other doctors and closed the door behind them.

'Sometimes, we are left with no choice than to painfully accept the hard news that comes our way. Sir, your wife and three children were involved in a fatal accident hours ago. Their saloon car was involved in a head on collision with a Land Cruiser that was being chased by a gang on motorbikes. Sadly, they were all crushed in the saloon car and their remains are in the morgue. The police managed to get this diary from the mangled car which made it easy for us to reach you. I am very sorry to break this news to you. Remain strong Sir,' the doctor consoled.

Radicus was dazed by the news and nearly hit his head against the wall but the timely intervention of the doctors saved the situation. He was visibly trembling and could no longer stand on his feet. He fell on the floor and cried.

'Forgive me, my family, because I have caused

this in my unrestrained anger. I defied the guidance of the Sages only to pursue the path of folly. I stubbornly fomented a great deal of trouble but this time, I have gone over the edge and cannot retrace my steps. My unruly temperament has ultimately courted me into the arms of horrendous reality and regret. I dug a dungeon of calamity for others only to fall into a pit of pain, misery and ignominy. Ah! I was eager to pull the strings of evil and now the noose is knotting round my neck. O God, my hands are tainted with grisly crimes, will I even find forgiveness in your sight?' Radicus lamented as he broke down uncontrollably. Freely and speedily, his tears flowed. Propgantus drove him home and had to be with him until the next morning.

'The police must not know that you are behind the demonstration. Even if the guys mention your name, we are going to deny it. They cannot produce any evidence to suggest you initiated it,' Propgantus told him.

'I cannot deny what I have done! Radicus replied.

'No, I am a lawyer so you must rely on my legal advice. If not you will find yourself in trouble. I am going to coach you on what to say and what not to say,' Propgantus insisted.

'My wife is gone. My children are gone. That is more troubling than what will happen to me. I must suffer the full consequences of my rash actions,' Radicus maintained.

***

Four suspects were charged with conspiracy to commit crime and were being processed for court. A great number of the youth involved in the protest were all rounded up, interrogated and cautioned before being granted bail. When some of them were asked to give their reason for participating in the demonstration, it came up that they were induced to be part of the demonstration by being offered money. The organizers had promised giving them money after the demonstration. Having sold their conscience for money, they were now to face the law.

The Commander dispatched police officers to arrest Radicus to ensure justice was served without delay. At 6:10am, they picked him up from his residence and whisked him off to their headquarters. He admitted being the mastermind behind the attack and was to stand trial with his conspirators in the coming days. His lawyers were unsuccessful with their bail application and had to leave him in police custody.

Propgantus rushed to a radio station to engage in misleading narratives when they could not secure bail for Radicus.

'Why do you arrest an innocent person who has nothing to do with this crime? Some unseen hands are behind this witch-hunting and it is a shameful attack on democracy. I am ashamed to be part of the IP. Are you so scared of internal competition and want to target us because we are gaining popularity? I am calling on all of our supporters to rise up and resist this repressive leadership,' he incited.

This display of barefaced mischief continued to feature glaringly in Masem politics. Some political communicators often muddied the waters to mislead those who were not privy to the inside story of contentious issues. Propgantus stunned many leaders of the IP who knew the facts of the case. His version of all the happenings flew in the face of the bare facts and so they listened to him with a pinch of salt. His conduct mirrored the death of conscience and birth of lies that had characterized the world of sham politicians.

A group calling itself 'Supporters of Radicus' trooped to the police station and chanted songs of agitation, demanding his immediate release. Comments made by Propgantus on radio had incited them to embark on this action.

'We will not go home until Radicus is freed. He is innocent. He had no hand in the demonstration. Free Radicus now!' they threatened but the police were determined to enforce order in spite of the ridiculous protests which often greeted their constitutional duties.

CHAPTER TWENTY

He had been in a coma for hours but when he began to moan and groan they knew he had eventually regained consciousness. He trembled in a spasm of pain and shook violently when two more medications were injected into his left thigh. The doctors held him firmly so he would not fall off the bed.

'What happened . . . ?' Susubribi struggled to ask but his eyes were still closed. Those were his first words since being brought to the hospital but the doctors were tight-lipped. They were not in a position to divulge any information related to the accident to him at this stage. He was not in the right frame of mind to handle what happened.

'His chance of survival is slim because he sustained severe cuts and has lost a considerable amount of blood. I think we must transfer him to a hospital with modern facilities,' the lead doctor told his assistants.

'It is the right thing to do under the circumstance so let's begin to get him out quickly. His wife must be told to start preparing,' one of the doctors added.

'Doctor! Doctor!' a nurse bumped into the meeting and alerted them of an emergency.

'What is it?' the lead doctor asked.

'He is gasping incessantly,' she replied as they run back to his bed. They gathered around him and did all they could to resuscitate him but their efforts were not yielding the expected results. He had relapsed into coma.

'The ambulance is here at last. We have to go now!' The lead doctor announced. Without delay, the ambulance sped off to a major hospital and he was rushed to an operating theatre upon arrival. After hours, the doctors announced that he was responding to treatment.

By 9am, the next day, there were rumbling lamentations and uproars in the air. Streaming tears could not be held back anymore because a great son of the land was no more. Masem was mourning. Susubribi did not wake up from sleep to see the morning light and a radio station had broken the sad news of his passing. Throughout the day, the airwaves buzzed with eulogies as people continued to pay glowing tributes to his noble memory.

Arrangements were made to honour his memory with a befitting burial. He had crossed the mortal bridge but his valuable contribution to his nation could hardly be buried with his remains. He had shown that it was possible to always prioritize national interests above extremely partisan considerations. The broader national interest had dictated his position on national issues irrespective of his political orientation and ideological leanings. He would vigorously debate his opponents and put forward his arguments without lies, deceits and insults. He would douse tensions with a great sense of humour and criticize his opponents based on issues. He practised politics without malice and insisted that justice must not suffer travesty. He was a quintessential nationalist, a principled politician, and a philanthropic change maker. Fighting for the downtrodden was the heartbeat of his soul and offering a helping hand to lift their social burdens were the things he eagerly dispensed his resources and exerted energies to accomplish.

The burial and funeral arrangements were swift. It was 12pm. The heap of sand around the tomb was about to be shovelled to cover the coffin that housed his remains. The procession kept swelling as mourners from far and near converged on Masem to bid him farewell. There was heightened silence and solemnity when the Sage approached to deliver his tribute before the interment. But for the chirping of birds, one would have thought that sound was dead. Everyone stood still in the dead quiet of the moment and nothing stirred.

'From various political, religious, ethnic and racial backgrounds, we have come to say *nante yie* (goodbye), the Sage began. 'If we had any grudges against you, it is now impossible to settle our differences with you. The lesson is clear; there is no second chance to reconcile with the dead so let's live in peace and harmony with all the living today. Let's trivialize our petty differences and eliminate our grudges. Let's pursue peace, love, reconciliation and forgive like Joseph; son of Jacob.

'Truly, there is no permanent station in life and such has been the human experience. Those who are dead were once here; we, who are here, will be gone one day. The throne will be left vacant by the occupant and in the final analysis; society shall render their verdict to posterity about who we were and what we did with our lives. Whether we lived for self or cared, whether we hoarded or shared, whether we strove for unity or division, for peace or for war, the story will be told just as the records will show. This thought should humble us all and guide our conduct in all our endeavours,' the Sage advised. He moved close to the grave and stared at the coffin for a while. Wiping his teary eyes with a handkerchief, he eulogized;

'To die, we all know, but when and how, we don't know,
Death is a mysterious reality,
With sweet melodies, man is received into the world,
With heart wrenching dirges, he is soon sent away,
We all owe death a debt we must pay one day,
At the tick of the clock each day,
We reluctantly hasten to meet that gloomy day,
When all loved ones would stand and say,
O why are you leaving us this way?
Safe journey Susubribi! safe journey my son!

Your virtues we shall extol,
You gave your all to the cause of humanity,
You played your part in building the nation,
Your deeds will be remembered for good,
Your presence shall be missed with fond memories,
Your impact will ring a bell in the hall of fame,
May your soul merit blissful transition!
May God grant you merciful judgement.'

Many had repressed their grief up to this point and burst out in uncontrollable cries when the Sage concluded. Leaders of the Religis and the Politicus came up to the Sage and accompanied him to his car when he was about to leave.

'Before we depart, let me tell you this,' the Sage said as they gathered around him. 'It is time for sober reflection. Susubribi is gone but his death should serve as a wake-up call to all of us. It should open our minds to the path of healthy politics and good neighbourliness. It should shake us from the illusion of complacency to make us weed out indecency in political competitions. Hatred or violence must have no place in our body politic and those who practise and encourage same are ignorantly plotting their day of shame. Let's call them out because such citizens are a threat to nation building,' the Sage warned.

CHAPTER TWENTY-ONE

The trial of Radicus was widely reported in the media and keenly monitored by a large audience who followed proceedings until the final determination of the case. In the early hours of the morning, a large crowd was seen descending on the court premises. Along the main entrance leading to the court, some of his supporters stood with placards bearing various inscriptions. Conspicuous among them was 'Free Radicus Now!'He had admitted complicity and pleaded guilty to the charges levelled against him. But Propgantus misled their foot soldiers and insisted Radicus was innocent and needed to be freed.

The courtroom had exhausted its capacity to hold the number of people who kept pouring in after going through rigorous security checks. By 9am, there was no space for even an ant to occupy in the packed public and media galleries. Key functionaries of the Politicus, especially, members of the IP were there in their numbers to witness the judgement. The journalists were eager for the verdict to write their headlines. All stood on their feet to welcome the stately presence of the Judge when the escort signalled her arrival. She was robed in a black gown with white bands falling over her collar. Her wig sat firmly on her head as her regal steps led her to the bench. The look on her face was one of dignity and solemnity.

All was set for the judgement to be delivered. The police escorted Radicus to the dock when his case was called. The urgency of the moment had completely subdued him and visibly stripped him of his aura of invincibility. "The hot-headed discovers sobriety only in moments of calamity," the words of the sage kept ringing in his mind. If only he had listened.

'Let there be order in this court! Order!' the Judge bellowed and banged the gavel on the desk. The auditorium became as silent as an ant hole. The courtroom epitomized immense discipline and striking sovereignty. This imposed some kind of decency and order in courtroom discourse and conduct. Rules of court required lawyers and their clients to be candid, measured and civil at all times or be cited for contempt for violating courtroom protocols. It was out of place for anyone to get up in court and speak without permission from a sitting judge. Had courtroom protocols been extended to public discourse, abuse of language would have lessened for decency and candour to colour national conversations.

'We must all understand that the stability of our society is hugely dependent on our total commitment to upholding the rule of law,' the judge stated. She continued, 'A little discretion on our part; a little patience, a little reasoning, and a little understanding, could save us all from a great deal of trouble. Citizens of Masem must understand that, whatever grievances or reservations there are; this is a civilized society where the law is supreme. You cannot exert militancy to get what you want! The law will always hit hard at those who put others in harm's way.

'Those who instigate violence promote lawlessness. They want to rule the law and do not want the law to rule. No, the law must rule for the good of all. Masem is a nation of laws and not of rowdy inclinations. It is only the rule of law that can guarantee a just and orderly society. Those who fight the laws of the land, ultimately fight themselves because the law will always be mightier than the muscular force of men. Radicus, you brought this upon yourself. The world does not birth problems for humanity; it is humans who create them. You are hereby sentenced to seventy years imprisonment,' the Judge pronounced.

The police came and handcuffed him. Why did he daringly pursue the path of belligerence to cause this irreparable destruction? This question crept into his mind as he pondered regrettably. It was a sad awakening to the voice of conscience which he had always ignored in the ugly noise of seething emotions. A second chance is seldom presented for one to right the wrongs. If there was any price to pay to rewrite one's story, Radicus would have paid it, but a broken egg can never be mended. The prison van was ready to transport him to where he was bound to spend the rest of his life.

He stood in the cage of the van and addressed his supporters who had gathered around to sympathize with him. They would have forcibly freed him if they had their way but the heavy security presence at the court premises allayed fears of militant intrusion. Radicus was close to tears as he addressed his supporters in a tone full of remorse.

'No matter the pain, no matter the bitterness, always, shun violence and resort to civil and judicious ways of seeking redress. If I had travelled the path of sanity, I would not have reached this untidy destination. I could have tamed my pride by dialoguing with reason but I relied on a false sense of power only to be conquered and humbled by the verdict of fate.

'I muffled the voice of reason by scorning sound counsel, only to find myself in the contemptible embrace of folly. I was swallowed up in fetish anger, but when the dust settled on the steam of my frenzied emotions, I realised that I have lost much than what I sought to gain. Will a man win with hatred or gain through violence?

'Hatred is like a bait that entraps the hearts of men to plot their own downfall. Violence does not build a nation, it ruins it. Hatred does not unite for good; it destroys. Tame your egos to avoid evil. Say no to politics of hatred, love all,' Radicus advised supporters. The van moved and made its way to the prison.

www.ingramcontent.com/pod-product-compliance
Ingram Content Group UK Ltd.
Pitfield, Milton Keynes, MK11 3LW, UK
UKHW022020190726
13853UKWH00005B/2033

9 789988 545581